FATHER
◆ ◆ ◆
GAETANO'S
◆ ◆ ◆
PUPPET
◆ ◆ ◆
CATECHISM

FATHER
◆ ◆ ◆
GAETANO'S
◆ ◆ ◆
PUPPET
◆ ◆ ◆
CATECHISM

A Novella

MIKE MIGNOLA &
CHRISTOPHER GOLDEN

ST. MARTIN'S PRESS
NEW YORK

FATHER GAETANO'S PUPPET CATECHISM. Copyright © 2012 by Mike Mignola and Christopher Golden. All rights reserved. Printed in the United States of America. For information, address St. Martin's Press, 175 Fifth Avenue, New York, N.Y. 10010.

www.stmartins.com

ISBN 978-0-312-64474-1 (hardcover)
ISBN 978-1-250-01859-5 (e-book)

First Edition: October 2012

10   9   8   7   6   5   4   3   2   1

For my son, Daniel, who is nobody's puppet.

—C. G.

For Carlo Collodi (Carlo Lorenzi, 1826–1890),
who forever altered my idea of what puppets
can (and should) be.

—M. M.

I

◆ ◆ ◆

THE VOICES OF THE NUNS from the convent of San Domenico rose and fell in a soothing rhythm, like the hush and crash of the waves against the nearby rocky shore. Nine-year-old Sebastiano Anzalone thought they sounded like angels. So beautiful were the voices that he found it difficult to imagine they could belong to the black-habited sisters who taught him writing and mathematics every day. Sister Veronica, perhaps; she had kind, sad eyes, and he could imagine her raising her voice in song. But Sister Maria and Sister Lucia were sterner and had little patience for the boys and girls that the war had left orphaned. Sebastiano did not really blame them—some of the children behaved like little devils—but he could not abide the curt chidings of the nuns, even when they weren't aimed at him.

His worn, battered mathematics book lay open on the small desk in front of him and he scribbled the answer to a question about how many lire he would have left if he bought a bar of chocolate. It was a strange question, because he hadn't held a bar of chocolate in his hands—nor any lire—since the Allies had taken Sicily from the Axis, killing his mother and father in the process. He missed chocolate, but not as much as he missed his mother and father.

Only three more questions to go. Sebastiano felt satisfied with his work and almost disappointed that when he finished this assignment he would have nothing more to do until tomorrow. Nearly all of the boys and many of the girls despised their school work. They would rather be out in the field behind the orphanage, kicking a football around, or down at the water's edge watching the fishing boats and warships sail past. Sebastiano didn't like the ships. If he let his gaze linger too long, he would want to know where they were going, and begin to wonder why he could not go as well, and there was no point in daydreaming about the kinds of wild adventures his father used to always promise to take him on. There would be no adventures for him.

No, unlike the other orphans, Sebastiano was content to sit at his little desk in the room he shared with three older boys, and to add and subtract and try to remember what chocolate tasted like. On an afternoon such as this, with the voices of the nuns rising from the church like the songs of angels, and the crashing of the sea, and the lovely smells of Sister Teresa's wildly colorful flower garden drifting through the window, he could almost forget the exploding sky and the screams and the tears from July and August, just for a moment.

And then the moment would pass and he would remember.

Sometimes remembering made him cry.

Sebastiano looked at his three remaining math problems and frowned. Flipping the page he saw that there were more, likely meant as tomorrow's assignment, and decided he would do them today. Adding and subtracting kept his mind occupied, and that was good.

Lost in his schoolwork, he almost did not notice when the voices of the nuns subsided, but then the momentary silence was broken by the deep, reassuring sound of the church bells, and he knew the mass had ended. Rising from his chair, he set down his pencil and went to the window to watch the sisters of San Domenico file out, filled with whatever private grace infused them during the mass said for them each Saturday morning. The nuns emerged in a peaceful stream of black habits and white wimples, of dangling crosses and rosaries wound about fingers, of kindly smiles to one another and conversations barely above a whisper.

Sebastiano blinked in surprise when he noticed a break in the parade of sisters—a man was amongst them, dressed in the cassock and surplice any priest might wear at the altar. Of course it was no surprise that a priest might be amongst the nuns, for wasn't a priest necessary for any mass? The surprise and curiosity that raised Sebastiano's eyebrows and made him lean on the windowsill for a better look came from the fact that he and the other children at San Domenico's newly christened home for orphans had been told that a new priest would soon arrive to take charge—not only of the church, but of the spiritual education of the orphans. Father Colisanti had died of a heart attack more than a month ago, and since then a number of the priests from local towns had shared the duties that a proper pastor would normally have fulfilled.

Sebastiano studied this priest, sure that he had never seen the man before. Young, thin, and dark-complexioned, he wore round spectacles that perched on the bridge of his hawk nose. His black hair was neatly combed but might need to be cut. It was strange. Normally, Sebastiano felt afraid of priests, for they seemed to him to carry a dreadful power, and when they looked at him he feared that God could see him through their eyes, and that the Lord would not be happy with what He saw. Sebastiano tried to be a good boy. He wanted to think that if his parents watched him from Heaven, they would be proud. Priests often made him want to find somewhere to hide.

But this new priest had a nice face. Sebastiano could see even from this distance that he smiled warmly at Sister Teresa as the two walked the path between the church and the orphanage together. The priest seemed comfortable, as if he felt at home.

"What do you think, Pagliaccio?" the boy asked.

He pulled his gaze from the open window and turned toward the small shelf above his tiny desk, where Pagliaccio lay sprawled on its side, bright red yarn hair dangling over the edge of the shelf along with its arms. Sebastiano frowned and hurried over to rearrange the puppet into a sitting position, arms crossed in its lap. *One of them moved you,* the boy thought. The boys who shared his room knew that Pagliaccio was his and they weren't to touch it. Sister Veronica had warned them after the last time, but apparently one of the other boys had ignored the warning. *Probably Giovanni.* He always seemed determined to do precisely the opposite of what the sister told him.

Sebastiano made a tutting noise, fussing with the puppet but unable to arrange it into a position that satisfied him. He picked up Pagliaccio instead and slipped his hand inside the wool sheath of the puppet's body, animating the arms and the head, making its face turn toward him as if responding to his presence. Sebastiano smiled.

"That's better, isn't it?" he said.

Pagliaccio nodded, then executed a silent bow. Sister Teresa had helped him with the sewing but he had painted the clown face onto the puppet by himself. The nose seemed too red to him and maybe too large, but mostly he loved Pagliaccio.

Now that he had the puppet in hand, his thoughts went back to the young priest, with his beak of a nose and long, skinny arms and legs that added to his birdlike appearance. Sebastiano took the puppet back to the window and bent to peek outside again. He was disappointed to see that most of the nuns had already vanished back to whatever duties awaited them, and the priest had also departed. But then he heard a low male voice and he glanced straight down, just in time to see Sister Veronica escorting the man into the orphanage.

"Do you suppose he's just another visiting priest?" Sebastiano asked the puppet. "Or is he the new pastor who is supposed to teach us about God and the Bible?"

The boy listened a moment, regarding the puppet earnestly, and then nodded. "Yes, I hope so, too. He doesn't seem so stern. It would be nice to have a priest who doesn't make us afraid."

Sebastiano thought that if they had a priest who would be kind, who would talk to them, he might not feel so alone. None of the other boys even tried to understand him and the girls only seemed to be amused by his presence when they could kick or punch him and get away with it. They were girls, which meant they giggled and hid their smiles behind their hands, and he had the feeling that they meant no harm, but still it made him sigh and wish for someone to talk to besides Pagliaccio.

"Though you *are* a good listener," he told the puppet, parroting something Sister Veronica had said many times. He liked that thought, that Pagliaccio was a good listener, and it made him think that as sharp as the nuns might be, they might actually be looking after him and the others, worrying for them in the prickly way he now associated with nuns.

The other children sometimes teased him because he did not hate the nuns the way most of them seemed to. The thought made his forehead crease in a frown as it occurred to him that the others—boys like Giovanni and Marcello especially—

wouldn't like it very much if Sebastiano acted too nice to the priest.

The boy held Pagliaccio close, staring out the window at the church and the sea beyond, waves crashing upon the rocks.

"Some of them are very angry at God," Sebastiano whispered to the puppet. "He took their families and their houses, like He did mine. But I know He still loves me, that He did not mean to hurt me."

The boy gazed at the puppet, worried and hopeful about the new priest at the same time. "They're angry at God, but they can't punish Him for it. Sometimes they punish me and some of the other kids instead."

Pagliaccio stared back at him, but made no reply.

2

♦ ♦ ♦

SISTER TERESA HAD AN UNDENIABLE DETERMINATION about her, but somehow she still managed a smile that held genuine sweetness. In that regard, the hazel-eyed nun reminded Father Gaetano of his mother. Though he'd been told that Sister Veronica filled the role of disciplinarian amongst the nuns at the convent of San Domenico—and now performed the same duty for the war orphans—Sister Teresa was the order's mother superior. She did not use the title, she said, because she did not like to set herself above the other nuns, but he wondered if there wasn't just a little bit of pride involved; a woman just forty might find it difficult to have other grown women calling her *mother.*

Indeed, it was unusual to have a relatively young woman acting as abbess, but the position was conferred by secret vote of the nuns in the community, so it was clear Sister Teresa had earned the respect of her sisters, even those many years her elder. Judging by the intelligence glittering in her eyes, Father Gaetano believed that the right woman had been chosen for the job.

"Something must be done," she insisted.

"Sister, I've only just arrived—" Father Gaetano began.

"I know, Father. And I hate to burden you with this before you've even had a chance to rest. I know that many new responsibilities await you, but that is my fear, don't you see? If I wait until you are mired in other concerns, you may forget us."

She smiled even more warmly, her habit proving insufficient to hide her beauty. Father Gaetano had been told that older priests developed the ability to ignore such distractions, but he had not yet reached that pinnacle of grace, and Sister Teresa's smile was persuasive. They had both given themselves to the service of God, but Gaetano Noe had grown up in a household with a smart, attractive mother and three beautiful sisters and had watched them manage the boys and men in their lives without any of those hapless males realizing how easily they were manipulated. He was not immune to Sister Teresa's charms.

"I understand," Father Gaetano said. He took off his round spectacles, wiped them on his cassock, and returned them to the bridge of his nose. "Lead on."

She had approached him after mass, before he had even had an opportunity to return to the sacristy and remove his vestments. Keeping him engaged in conversation, she had escorted him from the church and across the lawn to the rectory, which had been transformed into an orphanage during the Allied assault. Father Gaetano would be living there as of today, overseeing the boys' floor while Sister Veronica stood sentinel over the girls, but he had thus far seen only the front parlor—where he had left his suitcase and small valise—and now the kitchen.

Sister Teresa had promised to make him tea, but the moment she had put the kettle on the stove, effectively trapping him with her hospitality, she had opened up this new conversational front, which had surely been her purpose all along. Now Father Gaetano stood, sliding back his chair. Sister Teresa followed suit, but gestured at the already steaming kettle.

"Don't you want to wait for your tea?"

The priest scratched one finger along his proud nose. "I didn't actually want tea, Sister. We were engaged in a polite ritual, and while it is kind of you to offer and I am grateful, if we are going to work together effectively, perhaps it's best we dispense with such courtesies."

Sister Teresa gave a soft laugh, and then nodded. "I do like you, Father. I think we're going to get along just fine. And, next time, I'll even let you change your clothes before I drag you off on an errand."

Father Gaetano executed a theatrical bow, and then gestured toward the rear door, through which they had entered.

"Shall we?"

Sister Teresa crossed the kitchen and turned off the stove, moving the kettle off of the hot burner. "The front door will be quicker."

Curious now, he followed her out of the kitchen and along a narrow hall that led to the foyer, beneath a chandelier with half of its bulbs burnt out. During the war, nearly everything had become scarce in Sicily, and though the Allies now had control of the island, that seemed unlikely to change. More lights would go dark before they could begin to acquire new ones.

He'd come through the foyer when he arrived, so he had already seen the two rounded, ornate staircases that curved up either wall toward the landing at the top, and the children's rooms beyond. He had seen many of the orphans outside, some of the boys kicking a football while the girls watched, and others climbing on the rocks by the shore. There must be more, but he hadn't seen them yet. Tonight, at the evening meal, he would formally introduce himself to the orphans, and on Monday he would begin to teach them.

"Coming, Father?" Sister Teresa asked.

He glanced up to see her standing in the now-open doorway, awaiting his attention with a bemused look on her face.

"Of course," he said. "But you will have to give me a tour afterward. I'd like to get my things—such as they are—hung and put away."

Sister Teresa nodded in understanding. "Certainly. And I'm sure you must be exhausted. If you'd like to rest a while before dinner, I'll do my best to see that you're not disturbed."

"That would be heavenly," Father Gaetano said, thinking of the automobile journey the previous evening. He had traveled through the night to be sure he would be able to say mass for the sisters this morning. There was so much to do here, but the thought of a bed and a soft pillow was alluring.

"First, let's see to your troubles," he added, not wanting to seem callous.

Sister Teresa escorted him down a winding path that led north, away from the church and the converted orphanage, and from the village of Tringale. The church had been built at the turn of the century, when the village had outgrown the much smaller chapel that still stood at its center. Now the Church of San Domenico was the crown that rested atop the head of the village. When the people looked to the north, they saw the bell tower with its tall steeple, close enough for an easy walk to mass. Close enough for the explosions of war to shatter windows, for bullets to score the walls, for the wounded to be brought from battle and laid out on the floor in the shadow of the cross, where their blood ran in tiny rivers along the mortar between the stones of the floor. A diocesan administrator had told him the grim story when he had received the assignment as pastor. Dark things had happened here, and Father Gaetano hoped to bring new light to the place.

The path led from the rectory onto a property covered by olive trees and then to a clearing where the convent stood, gray and foreboding except for the vegetable garden that had been planted not far from the door. Though it was nearly November, somehow there were still a few tomatoes ripening there.

When Sister Teresa guided him around to the far side of the building, his heart sank at the sight of the damage to the convent. A portion of the third floor wall had been knocked away, and a small section of the roof had been undermined, drooping ominously. A severe storm might cause it to fall in, but all that the sisters had been able to do thus far was drape canvas—what looked to be the torn sails of fishing boats— over the hole.

"When did this happen?"

"The fifteenth of July, only a few days after the Allies began their assault," Sister Teresa replied, a new chill making her tone brittle. "Sister Annica was in her bedroom when the bomb hit. We . . ." She turned away from him. "We were able to pull the debris off of her, but there was nothing we could do. She succumbed to her injuries."

Father Gaetano stared at the canvas draped over the hole in the convent wall. A breeze made it billow slightly, and though he first thought of bedroom curtains, he could not help also thinking of a burial shroud. How could he convince more than two dozen orphans ranging in age from seven to fifteen that God loved them, that He had taken away their parents as part of His great plan for mankind?

"It will be repaired immediately," he said.

"It's been months, Father," Sister Teresa replied. "There was so much damage to the village—houses and shops destroyed, the schoolhouse nothing but debris—people have been so busy clearing the rubble that they've barely begun to rebuild their own homes. And building supplies are as scarce as everything else right now."

Father Gaetano frowned. He knew that his youth sometimes caused people to underestimate him, but there was power in the Roman collar and he knew how to wield it.

"I will speak to them from the altar at tomorrow's mass," he said firmly. "You and the other sisters minister to their spiritual needs. Without your guidance, they might well wander from the path of God. The very least they can do in return is to see to your safety. A few men, a few hours a day until it's done. They'll be able to see to their own concerns at the same time."

He turned to her. "Trust me, Sister. It will be done."

3

♦ ♦ ♦

SISTER VERONICA WATCHED the children file in for dinner, noting with approval the combination of excitement and nervous curiosity on their faces. Word had spread of Father Gaetano's arrival and they would naturally be wondering what changes in their lives might be heralded by his coming. Sister Veronica had already met him, but she felt herself plagued by the same questions. The lanky, awkward young man looked more like a scientist than a priest. It was good that he was not a handsome man, for that might have been a distraction for the older girls. *And the younger nuns,* she thought.

For herself, Sister Veronica was mainly concerned about what sort of teacher and administrator Father Gaetano would turn out to be. While he could not interfere in the lives of the nuns within the convent, as pastor of San Domenico he had authority over both church and orphanage. Sister Teresa seemed convinced that the young priest would fulfill his role as teacher and confessor to the students, but otherwise would leave the running of the orphanage to the sisters. Sister Veronica hoped it would be so. It had been difficult enough for her to coordinate the creation of the orphanage when she had the freedom to act without constraint. The newcomer's interference would make it that much more troublesome and complex.

When the battle for Sicily had begun, she and the other sisters had worked with the church's former pastor, Father Colisanti, to help wherever they could. They had nursed the injured while Father Colisanti performed the last rites for so many, Italians and Germans at first, and later for Allied soldiers as well. And when the battle was over and the Allies had taken control, they had helped bury the dead. Father Colisanti survived it all, only to suffer a heart attack mere hours after giving a final blessing at the funeral of the last of the war dead. It had been days before a priest from Gera could come and speak the same blessing for Father Colisanti, but at last the kindly old man had been given into the hands of God.

With no pastor, the sisters had been left to their own devices. Nearly every day, a priest from one of the neighboring villages had come to say mass for the people of Tringale and for the sisters of San Domenico, and in the meantime, the nuns had been busy gathering the children left orphaned by the long fight for control of Sicily, its strategic position in the Mediterranean making it a prize for either side.

Some of the children whose parents had been killed during the long weeks of battle had other relatives in the village who could take them in, but in too many cases the children were alone. Several had lost their mothers and had fathers who had gone off to war and not yet returned, their fate uncertain. With Sister Teresa's blessing, Sister Veronica had organized the nuns at San Domenico to give thirty-one children a place to sleep, warm clothes to wear, and three meals a day. Still mourning their own losses, the sisters had turned their grief into tenderness toward these children who had nothing and no one.

But it wasn't enough. Sister Veronica had been a teacher at a Catholic school in Palermo after she had first taken her vows. The school in the village had been destroyed and, while they could not see to the education of all of Tringale's children, she knew they had an obligation to cultivate the minds of the twelve girls and nineteen boys whom the Lord had put into their care. Born from chaos and tragedy, the orphanage had brought order to the children's lives.

Father Gaetano was an unknown variable, which made Sister Veronica wary. The nuns had achieved a certain balance through patience, hard work, and the grace of God, and she did not want that balance upset.

"Excuse me, Sister?"

She turned to see a curly-haired boy named Carmelo smiling pleasantly at her. He'd turned eleven the week before and she had given him a fisherman's cap as a gift. She had traded some fresh tomatoes from the garden for the secondhand cap, but it was in fine condition, and the boy had rarely taken it off since, other than during church and presumably at bedtime.

"What is it?" she asked, smiling to soften her features. Sister Veronica knew that her narrow features and high cheekbones could make her look stern even when she did not intend it. Her height could be imposing enough, so she tried to remember to smile around the children . . . though sometimes she wanted them to be wary of her.

"Do you know what's for supper tonight?"

"I'm told Sister Maria has made her fish soup."

Carmelo made a face, wrinkling his nose. "Again?" he whined.

Sister Veronica tapped the brim of his hat. "It's good for you. Besides, how can you be a fisherman . . . How can you be a Sicilian . . . and not like fish?"

The boy smiled. "I like baccala. Even calamari. But Sister Maria's fish soup is—"

"Ssshhh," Sister Veronica said, nodding toward the door to the back kitchen at the far end of the dining room. "You'll hurt her feelings."

Privately, though, she agreed. Sister Maria's fish soup was always very bland. It was the one thing the other nuns let her cook. They called it her specialty, but in truth it was a night off for the others, and amounted mostly to a stew of leftovers from whatever fish dishes had been made earlier in the week.

Abruptly, the children began to shush each other, and amidst the susurrus of their voices, Sister Veronica turned to see that Sister Teresa and Father Gaetano had entered the dining room. A pair of twelve-year-old girls, Concetta and Giulia, began to whisper to each other, apparently exchanging first impressions of the priest, but the rest of the children were standing at strict attention.

"Good evening, children," Sister Teresa began.

"Good evening, Sister Teresa," they chorused back.

"These long months have been difficult for all of us," Sister Teresa went on. "Each of us has lost someone we loved. The war came to our doorsteps and did a great deal of damage. But with the grace of God, we have already begun to rebuild our lives. The sisters of San Domenico have become teachers and caretakers. Our futures are intertwined with yours, and we thank God, for we see the opportunity to know you all and to help guide you on the path the Lord has set out for you as a blessing. Along the way, we will all face challenges, among them the loss of Father Colisanti. God called his servant home. I know Father Colisanti is even now singing with the hosts of Heaven. In his absence, we've had many kind and wonderful priests visit us, but the church of San Domenico needs a pastor, and you children need a theological instructor and a confessor."

Sister Teresa paused for effect. Sister Veronica tried to hide her smile at the way the children hung on her words. She envied her mother superior's command of the children, wishing they would pay even half so much attention in class as they were paying now. There had been much talk and much curiosity ever since it had been rumored that a new priest had been chosen for the church of San Domenico.

"Boys and girls, please give your attention and the warmest of welcomes to your new pastor, Father Gaetano Noe."

It was an invitation for the children to react, almost as if Sister Teresa expected them to applaud, but the children seemed to sense that clapping would be inappropriate. Instead, they turned to stare at the young, lanky priest with his round spectacles. For his part, Father Gaetano offered a nervous grin and then seemed to summon up the gravity that came along with his collar.

"Hello, children," said the priest.

"Good evening, Father," they replied.

He started out all right, Sister Veronica thought. Smiling in the right places, he told the orphans how much he looked forward to getting to know them and invited them to come and see him any time they wished. He tried to connect with the boys by talking about football and promised that they would spend enough time in church and talking about the Bible during class time that he would be happy to discuss whatever interested them. He appealed to the girls by mentioning a love of music and movies and a weakness for chocolate.

It should have worked, really. But these were children whose parents had been killed months earlier, taken by bombs or bullets or collapsing buildings, and they were wary about anyone new coming into their lives, no matter who had sent them on the errand. Father Gaetano might speak on God's behalf, but Sister Veronica knew the pain in these young hearts. The children had put their trust in God, and now they didn't know what to make of Him.

Sister Veronica and Sister Teresa exchanged a look. The mother superior saw it just as clearly as Sister Veronica, but it would have been inappropriate for one of them to interrupt, and Father Gaetano was going to have to establish his own relationship with the orphans, whatever that relationship might be.

Suddenly, the priest let out a quiet laugh. "I can see that you're all very bored with me already. Not the best way to begin, is it?" He threw up his hands in surrender. "Well, at least now there's no need for me to warn you that I talk a lot."

Several of the children laughed. Little Sebastiano smiled—he, at least, seemed charmed—and a few of them nodded, agreeing that they were bored.

"You're probably also hungry," Father Gaetano went on. "And I hear Sister Maria's fish soup is quite . . . memorable."

More of them laughed this time, looking around guiltily to make sure Sister Maria wasn't in the room. The priest took off his glasses and cleaned them with a kerchief from his pocket, a conspiratorial twinkle in his eye as he regarded the children again.

Maybe he won't have trouble with them after all, Sister Veronica thought.

"Dinner will be ready soon, I presume. Before we eat, do any of you have questions for me?" he asked.

Alessandra raised her hand. She was ten, but looked no more than eight, a slight little wisp of a girl with large eyes. Her hair hung across her face much of the time and she often used it as a veil to hide behind.

Father Gaetano pointed to her and asked her name, which the girl promptly provided.

"What's your question, little one?" the priest asked, smiling.

Alessandra fixed him with a pleading gaze. "Where is God?"

Father Gaetano spread his arms. "Why, He's all around us, of course. Everywhere."

The little girl's lip trembled, but she frowned and forced it to stop. "Is He there when I cry at night?"

The priest's smile vanished, his eyes filling with under-standing. "Yes. He is there with you."

"Then why doesn't He try to make me feel better?" Alessandra asked, her voice breaking.

Since he and Sister Teresa had entered, Father Gaetano had stood with the mother superior at one end of the room, as if it were a classroom rather than the dining room, creating a sort of invisible barrier between themselves and the children. Now Father Gaetano broke that barrier. He walked to Alessandra, who stood beside the table where she was assigned to sit for dinner, as all of the students did.

Father Gaetano crouched before her and reached up to touch her face. He looked into her eyes.

"Open your heart to Him and He will give you comfort," the priest said. "You will feel Him there if you have faith in Him. But that does not mean you will not cry, Alessandra. There will be tears. Your parents are with God, now, and He will take good care of them. One day, you will meet them again, but I know for a young girl that time seems very long from now. You cry because you miss them terribly, and that is only right."

Father Gaetano glanced around at the other children. Several of them were wiping at their eyes. Alessandra had been the one to ask, but they all felt the same pain. Some of them seemed to truly be listening, but other faces were stony, closed off from the priest's words, their grief still too mixed up with anger to listen.

"Let the Lord give you comfort," the priest said, returning his attention to Alessandra. "Sometimes you will cry and sometimes you will laugh, and one day not so very long from now you will find yourself with more laughter than tears, as your parents would have wanted it, and you will know that God is with you."

He stood up, clapping his hands. "But tonight is not a night for tears, my young friends. It is a night for good food and new friends."

Sister Veronica glanced again at the door to the back kitchen and saw that Sister Maria had emerged. Father Gaetano had noticed as well.

"Dinner is ready, children," the priest said. "Please, all of you, be seated and we will offer a prayer of thanks for this meal, for each other, and for the good sisters of San Domenico, who provide so much for all of us."

As the children sat, steepling their hands in front of them in preparation for prayer, Sister Veronica saw young Sebastiano Anzalone reach inside his sweater and produce the little woolen clown puppet the boy always seemed to have with him. She sighed inwardly. Sebastiano was a sweet-natured boy and a good student, and she hated to have to chide him, but she could not make allowances for him and not for others who might like to bring a book or a toy or other distraction to dinner. It was not appropriate, especially during prayer.

The boy settled the clown puppet into his lap, positioning it so that his hands were clasped over the puppet's hands, as if the two were praying together. Father Gaetano had not noticed, and Sister Veronica was grateful for that. She did not want him to begin with a poor impression of Sebastiano.

She waited until Father Gaetano had blessed the meal and they had all completed their prayer. As several of the sisters carried large pots out from the back kitchen, the eldest child at each table ladled fish soup into the others' bowls, serving themselves last.

Sister Veronica went down on one knee beside Sebastiano, holding on to his chair for balance. Her knees and back often gave her trouble, the years catching up to her.

"Sebastiano," she said softly.

The boy looked at her innocently, taking a moment to realize his mistake. Then he glanced away guiltily, tucking the puppet closer to his body, covering its head with his hands as if to hide it.

"What have I said about your little friend?" the nun asked.

"That I'm not to bring Pagliaccio to class or to meals," the boy said, despondent. "But I forgot, Sister. Really, I did. I wanted to introduce him to the new pastor . . . to Father Gaetano."

Sister Veronica let out a long breath. She didn't want to be cruel, but the boy needed to let go of some of his childhood illusions. He might only be nine, but the world had not been kind to him. The temptation to allow him to find solace in his imagination was great, but it would do him no favors.

"Father Gaetano will be too busy for such games," she said, and saw the boy flinch and glance at the floor, embarrassed or sad or both. "And the next time you bring Pagliaccio to the dining room or to class, I will take him away and you will not get him back."

"Not ever?" Sebastiano asked, glancing up quickly, eyes wide.

Feeling like the devil himself, and hating herself for it, Sister Veronica fixed him with a stern look. "Not ever."

Sebastiano hurriedly tucked the clown puppet into his shirt and sat up straight, waiting for his fish soup. Sister Veronica watched him a moment longer and then turned away, striding toward her own seat. She saw that Father Gaetano was engaged in conversation with some of the older students at his table, eliciting questions and even some laughs, and she wondered what sort of partner he was going to turn out to be when it came to preparing these children for the future. Some of them might be adopted, but in the aftermath of war, few families had enough for themselves, never mind enough to bring new children into a household. Many of them would be alone, now, until they could build new lives for themselves as adults, with paying work and a husband or wife and children of their own.

Father Gaetano had promised them more laughter than tears, but Sister Veronica feared that might be a hollow promise.

Innocence lost could never be regained.

4

◆ ◆ ◆

ON SUNDAY NIGHT, more exhausted than he'd ever been, Father Gaetano strode from room to room on the boys' floor, checking to be sure his charges were ready for bed. His shoes made a slap and scuff on the floor of the corridor as he wondered how many priests had once called this old building home. The faded aromas of cologne and cigars lingered, settled forever into the paint on the walls. A burst of laughter came from one of the rooms along the hall, and in such staid surroundings the happy noise was discordant.

Not just a rectory, he thought, studying the Christian images and symbols that hung on the walls. A cursory examination made it clear that this building predated both church and convent and had once been a private home. But even as a rectory, it had been more than that. Prior to the war, the pastor and several active priests had lived here, along with servants, but the number of additional rooms indicated other residents as well, and he suspected it had also been a home for retired clergy. It didn't feel like a place where children belonged, and he wondered if it ever would.

The first floor was made up of two parlors, two ornate

offices, the small kitchen where Sister Teresa had first made him tea, the enormous dining room, and the much larger cooking area, referred to as the back kitchen, where the nuns fixed the meals for themselves, the orphans, and the rectory's priests. A second kitchen was not uncommon in Sicilian households, and Father Gaetano suspected it had been built— and the dining room enlarged—when the building had first been turned into a rectory.

The girls had their rooms on the second floor and the boys on the third. The building had no attic; instead, the three small rooms under the gabled roof on the fourth floor had been used for storage, until the nuns had converted two of them into classrooms, breaking the students up by age for their lessons. Father Gaetano had been given a room on the third floor, to monitor the boys, and Sister Veronica had a room on the second floor, amongst the girls.

The priest had never had to oversee children before, but he was familiar with the mischievous minds of boys; once upon a time, he'd been one himself. So, while he wanted them to trust him, and he hoped they would like him, he knew that he would also have to cultivate a healthy fear of his ire. A stern word or look would not go amiss, if aimed correctly.

He had already checked two rooms, reminding the boys to say their prayers, as lights out would come in mere minutes. Now he turned into a third room, quickly reminding himself of the names of the two boys who shared the small, spartan space. Quiet, wounded Enrico lay on his bed, scrawling something in what appeared to be a journal. His roommate, Matteo, sat on the windowsill, staring out at the night. In the quiet of the room, Father Gaetano could hear the crash of the surf through the open window.

In the twenty-four hours since the priest had first met the orphans in his care, he had already learned that Matteo had an angry heart, a sharp tongue, and a penchant for mischief. But all of the rebellion he'd seen in the boy was absent tonight. He seemed weary and deflated, and Father Gaetano saw some of his own exhaustion in the face of this thirteen-year-old boy. The only sign of Matteo's troublesome nature was the unlit cigarette dangling from his lips, as if he'd meant to smoke it but forgotten. The young priest did not think he had ever seen anyone who looked so alone.

Enrico glanced up as Father Gaetano entered, but Matteo ignored him.

"Matteo."

The boy let his gaze linger on the night-dark window a moment longer and then turned. "Father?"

Father Gaetano gestured at the boy's cigarette. "Let's not get off on the wrong foot. You know you aren't allowed to smoke."

"The sisters smoke in the back kitchen."

The priest nodded. "I'm aware. But they are grown and you are just a boy. Smoking can affect your physical development. When you're older, you can smoke all you like. But even then, I'd recommend against smoking in your bedroom, surrounded by linens and blankets and draperies that might ignite with the merest speck of burning ash."

Matteo seemed to consider this, then nodded. "Sounds reasonable." He gestured with the cigarette. "But as you can see,

Father, I'm not smoking. Do you know how difficult it is to get cigarettes these days? Harder than finding a Coca-Cola. I'm saving this. One day, when they're not quite so hard to get, I'll smoke it. If I get in trouble for it then, it will be worth it."

Father Gaetano considered taking the cigarette away, but instead he smiled. "Fair enough."

Pleased, Matteo thanked him and slid the cigarette behind one ear.

"The bell for lights out will ring in just a few minutes," Father Gaetano told the two boys. "You should say your prayers."

Quiet, thoughtful Enrico closed his journal and sat up, studying him. "Who are we praying to, Father? Some of the other children say there is no God. Stefania says if he ever lived, he must be dead now, or he would not allow such horrible things to happen."

Father Gaetano sat on the edge of the boy's bed, fixing him with a reassuring gaze. "God still lives, Enrico. He has given us this world, but also the freedom to do with it as we wish. When men choose evil over good, we are breaking our contract with God. But He wants us to make better choices. He wants good men to rise up and drive away the evils of the world."

"So He has abandoned us," Enrico said, clutching his journal to his chest.

"Never," Father Gaetano said. "Surely you must know the story of the crucifixion. According to Matthew's gospel, Jesus cried out, 'My God, why have You forsaken me?' Though he knew that his suffering would open the way to Heaven for us all, that his pain would have an end, and that his sacrifice was necessary as part of God's plan—"

Matteo hopped off the windowsill, walking to his bed. "Just give it up for tonight, Father."

Stung, irritated at the interruption, Father Gaetano glared at him. "What?"

"Enrico's not the Son of God. Neither am I. We don't have some special destiny. What we've lost isn't some sacri-

fice that's going to save the world. Our parents, and Enrico's little sister . . . they're dead. What did the world gain from that? Nothing. And that's God's plan?"

The boy flopped on his bed, facing the wall, his back to both Enrico and the priest.

"Tell your bedtime stories to the younger kids, Father. Maybe they'll still believe in fairy tales."

Emotion roiled in Father Gaetano, fury and sorrow and guilt all churned together as he tried to sort through his thoughts and search his heart for some response. When the bell clanged in the corridor—Sister Veronica ringing it from the top of the stairs, just before she would go down and do the same thing on the girls' floor—he felt a flood of relief at the interruption.

"Lights out," he said. "But we'll discuss this more during our lesson tomorrow."

Matteo didn't reply, just kept his face toward the wall.

"Good night, Father," Enrico said softly, sliding under his covers.

Still, the priest felt he should speak. But all he could manage was a simple "Good night" before he clicked off the light. As he left the room he realized he ought to have told the boys he would pray for them, if they would not pray for themselves. Then he wondered why he felt the need to tell them. The prayers would be equally powerful whether or not Matteo and Enrico were aware of them. What did it matter if they knew?

Yet somehow it did. He needed them to know that God saw their pain. That He was listening, even if they did not receive the reply they longed for.

Walking down the hall, he reached the door to his own bedroom, which was opposite the stairs. It was early, yet— even for a priest who had to be up by five a.m.—but he felt weary to the bone and knew it would be best if he went to bed. As he paused, he heard a voice coming from the next room along, which was shared by the three youngest boys.

"Shut up!" one of them snapped.

Whispered argument followed, but he couldn't make out

the words even as he approached the door. He rapped once and then turned the knob, stepping into the moonlit room.

"Time to settle down, boys," he said kindly. "You know lights out means it's time for sleep."

"We're trying, but Sebastiano won't shut up," one of them muttered bitterly.

"Every night it's the same," said another. Giovanni, the priest thought. "Sebastiano keeps whispering to that stupid puppet till he falls asleep."

Father Gaetano frowned. He blinked as his eyes continued to adjust, until the warm, golden glow from the moon and stars was enough for him to make out details. The little one, Sebastiano, was only nine, a scrawny boy who lay on his side, knees pulled up in a protective posture. The head of a small, garishly painted puppet jutted from the place where he clasped it to his chest. It took a moment for the priest to recognize it as a clown, and he smiled. He'd always loved clowns.

"Sebastiano, who's your friend?"

The boy glanced away for a moment, then raised his eyes with a wary expression. "Pagliaccio."

Father Gaetano smiled, reached down, and ruffled the boy's hair. "Well, you and Pagliaccio need to get some rest, okay? Anything the two of you have to say to one another can wait until morning."

Little Sebastiano frowned. "It's not the same in the morning. He's not . . ." The words trailed off.

"Please go to bed, Sebastiano," Father Gaetano said.

"Yes, Father."

"I hate that stupid puppet," Giovanni rasped, pulling his covers up over his head.

Father Gaetano might have admonished him, but all three of the boys fell silent then. Any further comment would have been counterproductive. The goal, at the moment, was to get them all to sleep, so he took his leave, backing quietly out of the room and closing the door behind him.

"The little angels all sleeping?" a silken voice whispered.

He turned to see Sister Teresa standing at the top of the stairs, her face pale as alabaster in the dim light from the wall sconces.

"Or soon will be," Father Gaetano replied, struck by how the soft light and the late hour and the gentle whisper made her seem so much less like a nun and so much more like a girl. He'd had plenty of practice acknowledging feminine beauty and then studiously ignoring its allure. He cleared his throat.

"I believe you called them little devils at some point last night," the priest said.

Again, that lovely, weary smile. "They're all angels when they're sleeping, Father." Sister Teresa turned as if to go back downstairs, but paused, watching him. "I'm about to return to the convent. The other sisters are gone as well, except for Sister Veronica, of course. She and I were about to have a cup of tea and we thought you might like to join us. There are anisette cookies, freshly baked."

A flutter of alarm passed through him. "Not by Sister Lucia, I pray."

Dinner at the orphanage this evening had been stuffed sardines prepared Catania style. They were horrid. For those orphans wondering about the existence of God, Father Gaetano felt sure the stuffed sardines offered no new evidence in favor of belief, and perhaps much to the contrary.

Sister Teresa smiled. "Thanks be to God, no. Sister Franca does our baking, and she's a wonder."

THE ANISETTE COOKIES were as tasty as promised. Father Gaetano sat in the small kitchen of the former rectory, dunking the cookies into his tea as often as he bothered to sip from the cup. Though he talked with the two nuns, he enjoyed just listening to them as much as actually conversing. While the other sisters seemed deferential to Teresa's status as mother superior, it was clear that Sister Veronica held no such reverence. The two were friends, and the priest appreciated being allowed into the circle of their friendship, even if only for tea.

Soon enough, though, his weariness got the better of him. He had traveled all of Friday night, performed Mass for the sisters on Saturday before becoming acclimated to the grounds and being introduced to the children at the orphanage, and then spent today fulfilling his role as pastor. He had said two masses for Sunday, officiated at a wedding, and made a circuit through the village, visiting the sick and infirm and those who would never recover from the injuries they had sustained in the battle for Sicily. He had followed that long day with dinner amongst the orphans, attempting to entertain them, distract them from their grief, and heal their faith all at the same time. After dinner, he had been responsible for the disposition of the boys, making certain they all attended to their evening ablutions before lights out.

Now he slid his chair back. "Sisters, it was my pleasure to join you, and I am grateful for the tea. I'll give my compliments to Sister Franca in the morning, but I really must put my head down."

"Of course, Father," Sister Teresa said, brushing a few crumbs from her sleeve and standing as well. "You have your first catechism lesson with the children tomorrow, just before their lunch. If you haven't had time yet to prepare, I'm sure they will be just as interested to hear about your travels before coming to us."

"Thank you, but I'm sure I'll be fine. I thought, honestly, that I would start at the very beginning. Since they haven't all been here the same length of time, meaning some will have had lessons others have not, and since we have no idea which of them had parents who took the time to teach them about our Lord and His works, it seems best to begin with a clean slate."

The nuns nodded approvingly.

"I focused on the New Testament," Sister Veronica said. "The lessons of Christ seemed most useful when they first arrived, with all of their grief. But I confess there was little structure to what I was teaching them."

"You need compassion, then, not structure," Father Gaetano assured her.

"Well, I'm sure you'll have no trouble," Sister Teresa repeated. "With all of your other responsibilities, it's my hope that your time teaching the children will be a joyful respite rather than an additional burden."

Father Gaetano smiled weakly. He had prayed for the very same thing. Celebrating the liturgy of the mass, ministering to the sick, counseling his flock, hearing confession, and seeing to the repairs of the convent would take up the majority of his time, and he hoped to find respite in the company of the children. Each night before bed he wrote his sermon for the following day's mass, and now to that tradition he would add a few minutes to make notes and consider how best to teach the orphans their catechism. Not that he worried he would have any difficulty teaching the stories and messages of the Bible, but already in his time here the children had posed profound questions about the nature of God. They'd had their faith shaken by their losses and tragedies. Teaching them catechism would not be as simple as he had imagined.

5

◆ ◆ ◆

ON MONDAY MORNING, Father Gaetano woke just after five o'clock, peered through tired, slitted eyes at the predawn gloom and the rain pattering his bedroom window, and yearned for his mother's house, the warmth of his childhood bed, and the smell of hot coffee that always accompanied his older sister's calls to come down for breakfast. If it wasn't raining, his mother would be upstairs, hanging laundry on the clothesline strung across the balcony.

Laundry, he thought, lying there in his cold, unfamiliar bed, which was canted ever so slightly to the left, so that he had spent all night afraid he might roll right off. At home, his sheets had always smelled of fresh soap and sunshine.

The devil might be mankind's greatest enemy, but Father Gaetano firmly believed that the second greatest nemesis faced by any priest must be Monday. Even the most faithful members of the Lord's flock might find themselves able to rest after mass concluded on Sunday morning, but Sunday was a priest's busiest day.

Now, as he threw back the covers, still longing for the warm aromas of home, the ghosts remained, but he could not think of his own mother and sister at home in Augusta. He was no longer a boy, but a man. Not merely a priest, but suddenly a pastor and a teacher. Today he would have to fill all of those roles, but sometimes they felt like masks.

Much as he enjoyed the company of Sister Teresa and Sister Veronica, with most of the nuns, Father Gaetano felt as if he were playing a role. His father had devoted himself to his work, leaving Gaetano to be raised by his mother. She had been kind but demanding, and he had never doubted that she loved him. With the memory of his mother so firmly rooted in his heart, it was difficult for him to take a position of authority or superiority over the Domenican sisters. An older priest might have attempted to dominate them, but he didn't have it in him. Any assertion of authority, even simply walking amongst them and noting the deference they paid him, felt like foolish pretense. Like a disguise. But he knew he would get used to it.

Hours later, during his first catechism lesson with the orphans of San Domenico, the mask had been required again, but he had surprised himself with how well he played the role assigned. When Enrico and Matteo, both age thirteen, began to assault one another every time Father Gaetano glanced at a book or the easel he had set up to use in place of a blackboard, the priest took his ruler, strode to the boys, and slapped the backs of their heads. He promised that the next time, it would be the ruler against their knuckles. The boys learned their lesson quickly, but the stern theologian was only one of the masks he wore during the lesson. Gentle confessor was another. Demanding instructor. Passionate man of faith. He showed them all of those guises, each more a facet of himself than an actual mask.

None of his masks—none of his faces—seemed to inspire them to pay sincere attention. When they questioned the wisdom or power of God, or worse yet, His existence, Father Gaetano attempted to reassure them that God loved them in spite of their doubts. He read them the tale of Thomas, the apostle who refused to believe that Jesus had returned from the dead, but this only seemed to encourage the doubters. Though at least those who vocalized their doubts were students he could be certain were paying attention. Many of the children gazed out the window, watching the rain and waiting for the lesson to end.

Mondays, he thought. But he knew it wasn't just today. The burdens weighing upon these children would still be there on Tuesday, and every other day of the week. How could he get through to them? How could he restore their faith and teach them about God's love if they had turned away from him, making their grief a hard callus upon their hearts? The questions had haunted him for the past two nights, and he had awoken this morning with their ghosts still roaming the halls of his mind.

When Sister Veronica rang the bell in the hall, indicating the end of the lesson, Father Gaetano felt sure he was just as relieved as the children were. Perhaps more so. He watched them hurry from the room, eager to get down to the dining room to eat their lunch, and knew that though he could teach them their catechism, he needed some way to make them feel connected to the gospels and parables and Biblical tales, something that would cause them to drop their guard enough that they could begin to believe in God's love again.

But he hadn't a clue what that something might be.

6

MORE THAN TWO WEEKS PASSED before an idea finally occurred to him. Father Gaetano had worked his way through
most of Genesis, taught the orphans about Adam and Eve
and the serpent in the Garden, about the Fall of Lucifer,
about Noah and the Flood, and the promise that God had
made to mankind after the waters receded. In each case there
were parallels he could draw, ways to address the children's
pain and the fractured nature of their relationship with God,
but still their eyes were mostly dull, their gazes distant. If he
made them laugh, the laughter would quickly fade.

This failing troubled him, taking up residence in the back
of his mind so that he was never free of it. Even as he counseled a young wife frustrated with her husband's caprice, said
mass for the village, or performed sacraments for those too
old and infirm to make it to the church, he tried to imagine
some way to get through to the children in his care.

Late on a Wednesday morning, he accompanied Sister Teresa while she inspected the repair work being done on the
convent by men from the village. He had called for volunteers
from the altar during Sunday mass, and several had stopped

him afterward to offer their services, clearly prompted by their wives.

By the time Father Gaetano and Sister Teresa returned to the orphanage, the children were filing into the dining room for lunch. Delicious aromas filled the room and Father Gaetano relaxed with the knowledge that Sister Maria had not prepared the midday meal. Nothing she made could have smelled so delicious. He paused to speak with Sister Rosalia about Agata, who had just turned fourteen and wanted to become a novice in the order. Sister Rosalia believed the girl was sincere, but Father Gaetano felt that Agata was too young, and her embracing of her faith too fervent. After working so hard to attempt to restore the faith of the orphans, he hated to have to cast doubt on Agata's love for God, but he feared she was clinging to the idea of the order because she feared the uncertainty of her future.

"Give her a year, Sister," he said quietly. "You and Agata must both learn patience."

Sister Rosalia nodded. "Yes, Father."

He turned and glanced about the room for his seat. The priest had made it a habit to eat with a different group of orphans at each meal, except for Friday, when he dined with the sisters. Marcello raised a hand and Father Gaetano saw that a spot had been saved for him at the table. It surprised him. The boy had made strides in managing his anger and offering respect to those around him, but he was still struggling. Father Gaetano thought it a good sign.

"Good afternoon, Father!" piped Concetta, a wide-eyed twelve-year-old girl who never spoke during catechism but was always first to greet him outside of the classroom.

"It's still morning, Concettina," he said as he passed the table where she sat with four other girls. "So, good morning to you."

Concetta giggled. It pleased him every time one of the orphans laughed.

When he slid into the open seat beside Marcello, he saw that the boys were eating braciole, along with chunks of cheese and freshly baked bread. Even before his stomach could rumble with hunger, Sister Lucia appeared with a plate and set it down before him. He thanked her and reached for a knife and fork, but as he began to cut into the braciole, he was distracted by another soft giggle from Concetta's table. He glanced over to see that little Sebastiano had moved from his own table to sit with the girls. The way the boy sat, slightly hunched and protective, it was impossible to see what mischief was causing the girls' amusement.

Father Gaetano watched Sebastiano's animated expressions, saw the way the boy's arms moved back and forth, and even before he got a glimpse of the tiny, painted face of the clown, he knew Sebastiano was telling a story. Then he spotted the red nose, the bright colors, and he remembered the nine-year-old's favorite toy, the puppet. What did he call it again?

Pagliaccio.

The little boy was furtive, using the puppet to put on a kind of show meant only for the girls at the table, but Father Gaetano caught glimpses of it. The girls seemed entranced, and Sebastiano lit up with enthusiasm as he entertained them, a moment of joy unencumbered by grief. Such moments were so rare for the orphans that the priest felt a happy relief washing over him, a satisfaction he knew would be temporary but relished just the same.

When Sister Veronica appeared beside the table where Sebastiano worked his small bit of magic, Father Gaetano blinked in surprise, the happy spell shattered. The nun looked formidable and ominous, but must have seemed nearly a monster to Sebastiano, judging by the boy's reaction to her arrival. The moment he noticed her he froze, then flinched as if she'd raised a hand to strike him. He turned from her, attempting to vanish the puppet inside his threadbare sweater, but Sister Veronica reached down and plucked it from his grasp.

Sebastiano let out a strangled cry, the wail of a wounded animal, and reached for the soft fabric of the clown. Sister Veronica snapped a single word—the boy's name—and he froze once more. His expression contained such utter sadness, such terrible understanding, that Father Gaetano had begun to slide his chair back before he even realized he intended to rise.

The nun spoke curtly, but too quietly for the priest to make out her words.

"No, Sister, please!" Sebastiano begged.

Some of the girls at the table looked on with horror or sympathy, but others turned away as if wishing they were anywhere else. Father Gaetano forced a smile onto his own face and strode toward the table, leaving his lunch behind with Marcello. Others at nearby tables had begun to stare, their attention drawn by Sebastiano's plaintive tone. Near the door into the back kitchen, Sister Lucia looked on, lips pressed into a sour twist, tutting her disapproval, though of the boy or of Sister Veronica, the priest could not be sure.

"What did I tell you would happen the next time you brought your toy to the dining room?" Sister Veronica was saying as Father Gaetano arrived beside her.

Sebastiano, lip quivering, dropped his gaze. His hands fussed together in his lap as tears began to well in his eyes. He whispered some reply, too quietly to hear.

"What's that?" Sister Veronica demanded, cutting a side-long glance at Father Gaetano, as if troubled by his presence.

"You said you'd . . . you'd take him away *forever!*" Sebastiano said, voice crumbling on the last word.

Sister Veronica held the clown puppet hostage in her hand. Father Gaetano saw her grip on Pagliaccio loosen a bit, perhaps with regret. He studied the nun's eyes and she glanced at him expectantly, as if she thought he ought to explain his intrusion.

"Pardon me, Sister," he said. "If you don't mind, I'd like to have a few words with Sebastiano in my office."

She arched an eyebrow. "Right now, Father?"

"As I said, if you don't mind."

He tried to read her expression, saw curiosity and uncertainty and a bit of irritation, and then she exhaled, much of the tension going out of her. Sister Veronica could be strict with the orphans at times, but she was not cruel, and now he wondered if the look she'd given him before had been a plea for him to interfere, to find her a way out of having to enforce her threat of taking the puppet away forever. He felt sure the threat had been made out of frustration, but going through with it would be unnecessarily cruel.

"Of course, Father," Sister Veronica said, bowing her head slightly before turning to the boy. "Sebastiano, we will discuss this later."

Wiping at his tears, glancing around at the children who were watching in fascination—just glad it wasn't them in trouble—the boy stood reluctantly, but he had eyes only for Pagliaccio. The clown hung limply in Sister Veronica's grasp.

"I'll need that as well," Father Gaetano said, indicating the puppet.

Sister Veronica pursed her lips in hesitation, then held it out to him. As Father Gaetano took it from her, he saw a spark of hope ignite in Sebastiano's eyes.

"Come along, boy," the priest said, turning to stride from the dining room, his lunch forgotten.

Sebastiano followed as if he were a dog, and the puppet his favorite bone.

FATHER GAETANO SAT in his wickedly uncomfortable office chair, elbows on the desk in front of him, turning the clown puppet over in his hands, studying it. Pagliaccio was a strange creation, with space for the boy's fingers to work the head and arms, but also with legs like a marionette. Snags in the fabric showed where strings had once been attached.

He looked up at the boy. In the large, wooden, slat-backed chair opposite the desk, Sebastiano looked tiny and pitiful.

"Where did Pagliaccio come from?" Father Gaetano asked. "Did your mother make him?"

The boy frowned. "Oh, no, Father. I didn't have him before

I came here. When Mrs. Costa . . . she was our neighbor, before . . . when she brought me here, I wouldn't talk to anyone. It wasn't that I didn't want to. More like I couldn't, the way you can't talk in a dream, except inside your head. Do you know what I mean? You can think the words, but in a dream it never feels like you're actually saying them out loud."

Father Gaetano regarded him with fascination, and then nodded. *Smart boy,* he thought.

"One of the sisters gave him to you?"

Sebastiano shook his head. "No, Father. It was Luciano. One day he just came up and showed me Pagliaccio. He made him dance and I laughed, and then I could talk again."

"This Luciano. I don't remember him among the boys. Surely I can't have missed him. Did he have family come to claim him?"

The little boy smiled softly, his sadness slipping away. "Luciano wasn't an orphan, Father. He was the caretaker." Sebastiano's eyes sparkled with excitement. "He had a whole puppet theatre and a box full of puppets. When we first arrived he would give us a show every night and make us laugh. Sometimes the shows were a little scary and I would hide my eyes and the big boys would tease me, but that was okay. I didn't mind, because Luciano's shows were so much fun, and the puppets didn't like the older children anyway. They would visit us little ones after the lights went out when we were supposed to be asleep, and they would dance and tell us stories and teach us songs. I would be so tired those mornings that it was hard to open my eyes and Sister Teresa would think I had been up all night crying, but I wasn't, and—"

"Just a moment," Father Gaetano said, holding up a hand to halt the boy's rapid-fire recollections. "The puppets would visit you after lights out? Luciano would come and do another show when you were meant to be sleeping?"

Sebastiano rolled his eyes, but out of amusement rather than disrespect. "No, Father. The puppets would come."

Father Gaetano smiled. The caretaker had been a clever man. The puppets had visited the younger children at night, but not the older ones, obviously because the older ones would not have been taken in by whatever sleight of hand the man had used to make the puppets' "visits" seem real. He nearly revealed the truth, but then thought better of it. The memory was such a cherished one that he did not want to steal it from the boy, or even to challenge it. Where was the harm in letting him believe the fantasy?

"What became of Luciano?" the priest asked. "Was he lost in the battle?"

Sebastiano frowned and shook his head. "No. He was old, Father. Old enough that his wife was already dead, but he had a grown-up daughter, who had a husband and a baby. Giacomo said he heard Sister Teresa telling some of the other sisters that Luciano's daughter's house was wrecked by a bomb and her husband died and she and her baby were going to live in Messina with the baby's other grandparents. Luciano didn't want to stay here if his daughter was leaving, so . . ."

The boy shrugged.

"And he gave you Pagliaccio before he left?" Father Gaetano asked.

"I always liked Pagliaccio best," Sebastiano said. "The morning after Luciano left, I woke up and Pagliaccio was sitting on my pillow. He said Luciano had meant for me to have him, and he wanted us to be friends. Of course I told him we were already friends," the boy finished proudly.

"Of course," Father Gaetano said, offering an indulgent smile.

He was thinking about the way Luciano had made the children laugh, made them forget their grief for a time, and the way that the girls at lunch had been so entranced by the small show that Sebastiano had put on for them.

"Sebastiano, do you know what became of the puppet theatre after Luciano left?"

The boy frowned, nodding grimly. "Yes. Father Colisanti never liked the puppets. I don't think he liked Luciano much, really. He told Sister Veronica to throw it out or give it away, but she told us kids that it was too beautiful to throw away and she was going to store it in the basement instead. I guess it's still there."

"Excellent," Father Gaetano said.

His thoughts were racing ahead, so that it took him a

moment to realize that, his story told, Sebastiano had remembered that he was in trouble and was staring longingly at the clown puppet that now lay on the priest's desk.

Father Gaetano slid the puppet over to the boy, and Sebastiano's eyes widened.

"Really?" he said with a grin. "I can have him back?"

"Better than that," Father Gaetano said. "I have a plan, Sebastiano, and I'm going to need you and Pagliaccio to help me with it."

The boy sat up straighter, chest filling with pride, and held the puppet in front of him as though they were both at attention.

"You can count on us, Father."

7

THE ONLY ILLUMINATION in the rectory basement came from four single bulbs that dangled from the ceiling on cables. Three of them flickered on when Sister Veronica hit the switch, though the one nearest the bottom of the stairs stayed dark.

"I must have that fixed," she said, glancing over her shoulder at Father Gaetano, and then beyond him at Marcello and Giacomo. "Perhaps you boys would attend to it later?"

"Yes, Sister," Giacomo said.

Marcello said nothing. His gaze shifted past her and he cocked his head to peer down the steps, as if he expected someone else to be waiting for them down there. The boy seemed strangely reticent, nothing like his usual swaggering self. Almost skittish.

"It's warm," Father Gaetano said.

Sister Veronica felt it as well, the warm, humid exhalation of the basement. In the summer, it felt cooler downstairs, but as soon as fall arrived, the temperature dynamic shifted and the furnace came on, and it always felt stuffy and claustrophobic and humid down there.

"The walls seep a bit," she admitted. "Groundwater, I've always thought. And the salt air is no friend to the mortar of the foundation."

She started down the stairs, feeling their familiar shift underfoot, hearing the usual creaks of old wood and loose nails. The musty, dusty odors of the basement embraced them as they filed down, the four of them descending and then turning right, at Sister Veronica's guidance. As many times as she had been down here, most of the things stored in the basement were unknown to her. There were old crates and shelves full of household items. She spotted a broken chandelier, apparently stored for future repair that would never arrive.

"It's just there," she said, pointing to the far corner, where a gray sheet that had once been white was draped over a large wooden frame. "Father Colisanti never approved. He said Luciano's puppet shows were a distraction, that they disturbed the inner search for God's peace that is so important for the orphans. Sister Teresa felt they needed laughter almost as much as prayer, and so he allowed it. But when Luciano left . . ."

Sister Veronica gestured at the draped sheet. "Well, here it rests."

Father Gaetano nodded, already thinking ahead to where he might put the puppet theatre in the room where he taught catechism lessons. He stepped past Sister Veronica, grabbed a fistful of the sheet, and tugged it loose. The fabric hissed across the wooden frame as the theatre's shroud slid free and pooled on the ground. Dust rose into the air, eddying on invisible currents, swirling in the dim glow of the nearest bare bulb.

The puppet theatre stood four and a half feet high. The molding around the opening—the puppets' stage—was ornate and lovely, a miniature version of some grand Italian theatre, and the small curtains that hung across the stage appeared to be genuine velvet.

"It's beautiful work," he said.

"Luciano made it himself," Sister Veronica said. "Carved all of the intricacies and painted it, just as he made all of the puppets."

Father Gaetano frowned and glanced about. "Where *are* the puppets?"

But even as he asked the question, he noticed the crate set atop an old, cracked sewing table a few feet away. In the drifting, settling dust, the gold filigree around the edges of the lid seemed strangely bright.

"There you are," Sister Veronica said, confirming what he already knew.

Father Gaetano heard the scuff of shoe leather and glanced back to see that Marcello had retreated a step back toward the staircase. Giacomo stood with his hands in his pockets, but his chin was raised with curiosity as he looked on. Marcello, on the other hand, shifted his gaze around the basement, looking at everything but Father Gaetano or Sister Veronica.

Whatever troubled the boy, Father Gaetano would have to inquire about it later. He had the impression Marcello would not want to discuss it in front of others.

He went to the crate, pausing as a sneeze overtook him. Sister Veronica and Giacomo quietly wished God's blessing upon him as he reached for the lid. At some point, perhaps while it was being shifted from one location to another, the lid had been jostled so that it did not fit snugly. Father Gaetano dragged the crate down off of the sewing table, grunting at the surprising weight of the large, ornate wooden box, and set it down nearer the pool of light, for closer inspection.

Setting aside the lid, he glanced inside, and his smile broadened. Though the contents were partially in shadow, he could make out many members of the cast of Luciano's puppet show. Pagliaccio the clown might have been young Sebastiano's favorite, but he was among the simplest of the caretaker's creations. The puppets were a lovely, brightly colored menagerie of heroes and monsters, their strings wound carefully around the wooden handles from which they would dangle during a show. He saw Hercules, Roland, Peter and the Wolf, Punch and Judy, what appeared to be musketeers, and at least two witches.

L'Opera dei Pupi was a great tradition in Sicily. Father Gaetano was not one of the cantastorî. He had never spent time as a troubadour, and he had no intention of singing during his catechism lessons, nor turning Biblical tales into opera. Yet he knew these marionettes would capture the children's attention.

He breathed in inspiration along with the dust, and when he sneezed again, it ended in a small laugh. In his mind's eyes, he could already see the ways in which he could alter the puppets for his purposes, could already feel the stories he wanted them to tell on the tip of his tongue.

Sebastiano would be his assistant. It would fill the boy with such joy, and together they would teach the orphans their catechism. Along the way, Father Gaetano felt sure, they would begin to understand the gift of free will and God's love for man, as well as God's hope for mankind.

"Perfect," he said, sliding the lid back into place and standing up, brushing at the dusty knees of his trousers. "They're perfect."

"The children will certainly enjoy having them back," Sister Veronica said with a smile, obviously pleased.

"All right," Father Gaetano said, turning to the boys they had brought into the basement. "Giacomo, help me with the theatre. Marcello, you carry the puppets up—"

"No."

Father Gaetano blinked and looked up at Marcello, who was shaking his head. He seemed about to explain himself, but then he moved quickly over to the theatre, putting his hands on it, a defiant, determined expression on his face.

"We'll carry the theatre up, Father," he said, a kind of plea in his voice.

"What are you—" the priest began.

"He doesn't like them," Giacomo said, nodding toward the crate.

A ripple of unease passed through Father Gaetano and he glanced at Sister Veronica, who looked very cross.

"Marcello," she said curtly.

The boy wouldn't look at her. Whatever had happened to the quick-witted, arrogant boy Father Gaetano was used to?

"It's all right, Sister," the priest said. "Giacomo, help Marcello."

The other boy nodded, took the unmanned end of the

puppet theatre, and moments later the ornate frame was being carted up the stairs, turned at odd angles in order to fit in the narrow stairwell.

"I'll see to the lights," Sister Veronica said.

Father Gaetano thanked her, bent, and lifted the crate. Again it struck him that it was strangely heavy, even taking the dense wood and carved lid into consideration. The puppets were also partly wood, and apparently their delicate appearance was misleading.

As odd as he found Marcello's behavior, as lugged his burden up the stairs, he began to think again of the ways in which he might use the puppets to teach his lessons, and his smile returned. His eyes itched from the dust, and he sneezed again.

"Bless you, Father," Sister Veronica said.

Behind him, she turned out the lights.

8

♦ ♦ ♦

SEBASTIANO FELT TROUBLED. He had Pagliaccio tucked
into a pocket as he bent over the work table, using a fine-tipped
paintbrush to create the illusion of a thick black beard on the
puppet who had once been Hercules. He wasn't Hercules anymore; Father Gaetano had seen to that. Dark yarn on his head
gave him a shaggy mane of hair and he held a club in his right
hand. Really, the club was a wooden peg from a cribbage
board, and Sebastiano felt proud that he'd thought of it. Father
Gaetano had grinned and ruffled his hair when he'd made the
suggestion. But the lightness in the boy's heart at that moment
had given way to worry.

He stepped back from the table to examine his handiwork,
allowing himself a moment of pride. When Father Gaetano
had told him that he could help with the puppets, he had never
imagined that the priest would trust him with something as
important as the beard. Repainting the puppets' clothes, yes,
but the marionettes' faces were the most important part, and in
transforming the Hercules puppet into Goliath, a mistake with
the beard would ruin everything. It would be a distraction
from the story Father Gaetano would be telling, and—worse,

by far—if the others found out it had been his mistake, they would tease him horribly.

But he hadn't made a mistake. He might only be a little boy, but he knew the difference between a good job and a sloppy one, and he'd done a good job.

"Excellent work!" Father Gaetano said, appearing just behind him.

Sebastiano jumped, shuffling a step away even as he turned to face the priest, worry rippling through him again, prickling at his skin.

"Thank you, Father," he said.

But the priest saw his hesitation, and must have also recognized the concern that weighed upon him.

"Is something wrong, Sebastiano?" Father Gaetano asked. "You seem . . . unhappy. I thought this work would please you."

"It does," the boy said quickly.

He liked the whir of the sewing machine and the rhythm of its foot pedal as Father Gaetano created new clothing for some of the caretaker's old puppets, rather than repainting them. In his mind, he could already see what the puppets would look like when they were finished, could imagine the way they would sound when all of their voices were Father Gaetano's voice. As much as he liked the priest, catechism lessons were boring. Puppet shows would be much better.

"Is it only that I startled you, or is there something else?" the priest went on.

Sebastiano shook his head, forcing a smile. He could not

tell if Father Gaetano believed him or not. The priest watched him a moment, then gave a small shrug and turned to the worktable, where the Goliath puppet lay with its painted beard drying. Father Gaetano picked it up and examined it, a small smile of approval touching his lips. He nodded in satisfaction, and that made Sebastiano feel good.

"This will be perfect," he said. Which was nice, because nobody had ever told Sebastiano that he had done anything perfectly.

The priest walked the puppet to a side table and set it down with several others. He would be doing the finishing touches there, untangling the strings and making any fine-detail changes to the faces. The workroom had once been the province of the caretaker, but there was no caretaker left to defend his territory. Sister Teresa had told them that one of the old priests who had lived in the building before the war had done much of the mending for the others, a skill taught to him by his seamstress mother, and they had found the sewing machine still in excellent condition, covered beneath a sheet to keep the dust off of its workings. Father Gaetano hadn't had a seamstress for a mother—Sebastiano guessed that the moment he saw the first piece of puppet clothing the priest had sewn together—but he managed well enough.

Most Sicilian marionettes were painted wood, but Luciano had made his puppets in a variety of ways, with wood and cloth and paint in whatever combination he felt suited that particular character.

Sebastiano watched as Father Gaetano studied the Goliath

puppet, where it lay with the others. He wondered if the puppet had done something it wasn't supposed to.

"What do you think?" Father Gaetano asked. "Should he have a belt?"

The boy pondered this a moment, then nodded. "Maybe just a bit of twine."

"Good idea, but I'll get to that in a moment, while I'm finishing his clothes. Meanwhile, how would you like to start work on the animals for Noah's ark? The wolf could be a tiger easily enough. And some of the monsters Luciano made—"

"Are you going to use them all, Father?" the boy blurted, unable to contain the question another moment.

Father Gaetano frowned. "The puppets, you mean?"

Sebastiano nodded vigorously.

"Well, I'll probably . . ." the priest began, and then he blinked and inhaled deeply before letting the air out, eyes narrowing. "You're concerned about Pagliaccio."

Another urgent nod. It made Sebastiano's neck hurt, but he couldn't help it. He felt like all of the muscles in his body were locked up tightly, the ones in his throat worst of all, for they wouldn't let another word out until he had his answer.

"I'll be using all of the caretaker's puppets eventually," Father Gaetano said. "With Luciano gone, they belong to the orphanage now. To San Domenico. But Pagliaccio doesn't belong to anyone but you, Sebastiano. He's yours, and I would never try to take him from you."

Sebastiano smiled so wide that his cheeks hurt. All of his worry evaporated, replaced by a merriment he had previously only felt on Christmas mornings, and never had expected to feel again after losing his parents. This fear had been weighing on him, but with it now removed, he could allow himself to take real pleasure in working on the other puppets, using his imagination.

He plucked Pagliaccio from his pocket, still grinning, and as he looked at the clown puppet, it seemed to him that the smile sewn into that cloth face seemed wider than before, a few extra stitches added to indicate Pagliaccio's joy at being able to stay himself. To stay with Sebastiano.

"Did you hear that?" he asked the clown puppet.

Pagliaccio did not reply, but the boy knew he was only being shy with the priest in the room.

"All right," Father Gaetano said. "I'm going to finish with Goliath. Why don't you go through the box and see which puppets you think would make good animals. We need at least four, I'd think. A lion, a tiger, a giraffe, and a zebra. If there's something big enough to be an elephant, that would work, too."

"Yes, Father," Sebastiano said.

He raced to the puppet box. Its heavy lid had been removed and set aside, and as the boy drew near to it, he thought he heard a faint scratching noise. With a frown, he glanced around, wondering for a moment if mice or rats had made their way into the workroom. Then he knelt by the box, bending curiously to look at the puppets piled within.

They had been all a jumble before. Now each and every one lay faceup, as if silently yearning to be next out of the box.

9

IT WAS NOT UNTIL the following Monday that Father Gaetano introduced the puppet theatre into his catechism lessons. As a boy, he had enjoyed carving wood and had learned how to play the violin, so he considered himself reasonably dexterous. Working the marionettes' strings without getting them tangled, and in such a way as to make them seem to walk or bow—or at least face one another while he gave them voices—had required days of practice, and still he was a poor excuse for a puppeteer. But his skills as a manipulator were not as important as the stories he wanted to tell, and so he forged on, and vowed to continue to improve.

A light rain fell outside, and the weather had turned cold. The priest knew that to those in some parts of the world, a fifty-degree day might be considered quite warm, but in Sicily—especially with the wind and the clouds and the drizzling rain—fifty degrees brought a litany of complaints. He had met a fellow priest from Norway the previous year, and the man's description of his home country's climate had caused Father Gaetano to make a silent vow never to visit the place.

"Are you ready?" a voice asked.

Father Gaetano turned to see Sister Teresa standing in the open doorway of the converted classroom. A spot of brightness and warmth bloomed in his chest and he felt himself grinning, before quickly extinguishing that unfamiliar spark he had begun feeling more and more often in her company. He was a man of the cloth, and she a bride of Christ. Any romantic feelings he might develop were mere foolishness. But he was always pleased to see her.

"Ready? Not at all. But I am committed to a course of action."

"Ah, well, that's almost as good," Sister Teresa said. She seemed to enjoy teasing him, now that they knew each other a bit better.

"Will you stay for the show?" he asked.

"Won't that make you nervous?"

"More nervous than I already am?"

Sister Teresa frowned. "To perform for children? Why should you be nervous?"

"In such moments, we are reminded that we are still only children ourselves, in our hearts," Father Gaetano said.

She nodded. "I suppose we are. But you have nothing to worry about. The children love the puppets and are excited to see what you've done with them. It's all they're whispering about today."

"Oh, excellent. You do realize that makes me even more nervous?"

"You'll be fine, Father," Sister Teresa said.

They heard footfalls from the corridor then, and Sister Teresa turned to let young Sebastiano slide past her through the door. The boy looked around the room as if it were Christmas morning and he sought the bounty Father Christmas had left behind. His eyes lit up when his gaze found the shape of the puppet theatre, draped with an old blanket, and the ornate box that sat uncovered beside it.

"Good morning, Sebastiano," Sister Teresa said, amused, although the boy had ignored her presence entirely.

"Huh?" the boy said, turning to glance at her. "Oh, good morning, Sister Teresa." He turned to Father Gaetano. "Can I be Goliath?"

The priest shook his head. "I'm afraid not. But next week, when it's time for the story of Noah, I'll let you be some of the animals. You'll have to practice tiger and lion sounds."

Sebastiano's momentary disappointment vanished at the introduction of this idea, and he nodded quickly, brow furrowing in thought, perhaps already working out how to make the roar of a lion sound different from that of a tiger. His excitement was contagious, and Father Gaetano hoped that the other students would feel it as well.

They began arriving moments later, trickling into the room in twos and threes. Many wore curious expressions, some even eager, and the younger children whispered to one another and glanced at the blanket-covered theatre with a kind of happiness that verged on delight. Father Gaetano felt his chest swell with emotion. Every one of these children had survived horrible loss. They ought to have been in a real school, with other children their own age, not lumped together like this. Wrapped inside of their grief was a core of resentment at the things that had been taken from them—innocence, love, happiness now and in the future, an identity based on family instead of tragedy—but today, at least, he thought he might be able to give them all a reason to smile, and to forget. If only for a moment.

Remembering Sister Teresa, he glanced at the doorway, but saw that she had gone. Despite the necessary chasteness of their friendship, he couldn't help feeling disappointed. He would be more intimidated by the prospect of performing if she had stayed, but he did like the idea of making her laugh. She had a wonderful laugh.

"All right, children," he said. "Please take your seats."

"Tell us about the puppets!" one girl said.

"Puppets," an older boy groaned, rolling his eyes.

But when Father Gaetano removed the blanket covering the theatre, pulling it away with a flourish worthy of a magician's cape, all of the children watched with rapt attention. He did not explain, presuming many of them had heard of his foray into the dusty basement already. Instead, he simply stepped behind the theatre, nodding to Sebastiano, who ran up to assist him with the curtains.

At the priest's signal, Sebastiano slid the curtain back, and the show began.

"Welcome, children, to Father Gaetano's Puppet Catechism," he intoned. "Today, we present the story of David and Goliath!"

HE STRUGGLED WITH THE STRINGS at first, wishing for the talent that would have allowed him to create a genuine illusion out of his marionettes. Though he had practiced, he still tangled the puppets together several times, and the children laughed each time he paused to extricate wooden limbs from one another. Some snickered, but that was to be expected. The older ones, both boy and girls, had adopted a general air of sophisticated disdain typical of children in their teens forced to spend time with younger kids . . . or with adults . . . or, really, with anyone at all.

Father Gaetano glanced up during these quick, delicate disentanglements, and from time to time during the performance itself, just to make sure that he had his audience's attention. One of the girls, twelve-year-old Giulia, looked askance at him, but he could not decide if she disapproved of his skills or of the very idea of being taught through puppetry.

As he went along, however, he warmed to the story and to the art of telling it, and his fingers found a dexterity they hadn't had before. Yes, the David puppet appeared to be having some kind of seizure rather than using a slingshot to attack Goliath, but the voices he gave them told the story, as did the sudden collapse and death of Goliath and the cheering of the Israelites—represented by several puppets Sebastiano dangled in front of the proscenium and the cries of victory the boy mustered. A few of the children joined in, cheering the death of the Philistine giant.

Father Gaetano could not suppress a flush of pride, though he knew he would have to find it in his heart to be penitent about it later on. He had engaged them. They had paid attention to the story. From here, could he not branch out to explore other Bible stories from the Old Testament? He believed he could. There were so many lessons he wanted to impart to them.

But as he carried the marionettes toward the box—strings wound carefully around their handles—he glanced out at the children again and saw one face that wore neither a smile nor a disapproving frown. Marcello, who had helped him bring the puppet theatre up from the basement, stared at the priest with unblinking eyes. The boy looked almost as if he were holding his breath. He sat straight up in his seat, pale and silent, hands folded in front of him. His fingers dug into the skin at the backs of his hands; this was not prayer.

"Marcello?" Father Gaetano asked.

The boy flinched as if the priest's voice had been a thunderclap. Only when Marcello glanced up, fixing his gaze anew, did Father Gaetano realize that the boy had not been focused on him after all, but on the marionettes that dangled from their strings.

Marcello wetted his lips with his tongue. He tried to force a smile, and it failed miserably. Father Gaetano placed the puppets back into their box, taking the others from Sebastiano and packing them away, and then he slid the cover into place. As he did, he noticed Marcello sinking deeper into his chair, his former rigidity gone, and he remembered the boy's unwillingness to carry that box up from the basement. Marcello had avoided that duty, recruiting Giacomo to help him heft the theatre instead.

The boy was afraid. But this didn't seem to be the time or place to ask him why; it would only embarrass him in front of the others. Father Gaetano had seen both children and adults who suffered from irrational fears of the most mundane things, from traveling by boat to swimming in the ocean, from neckties to umbrellas. Perhaps, he thought, Marcello had such a terror of puppets. *Yes. That must be it.*

Now, as he glanced at the boy again, Marcello would not meet his gaze.

"Father?" asked Concetta, raising her hand.

"Yes?"

"If King David is Sicily, then who is Goliath meant to be? America, or the Nazis?"

Father Gaetano blinked in surprise, intrigued by the question.

"Who said that King David—though he was not king at this point—who said that David represented Sicily?"

Concetta smiled shyly and gestured to her left. "Giulia."

The other girl shifted awkwardly in her chair. "I didn't say David was Sicily, just that he was like Sicily, going up against monsters stronger than he was, and coming out all right in the end."

Giacomo barked a dismissive laugh. "All right? You think we're all right?"

Father Gaetano held up a hand, giving the boy the stern look that always quieted the children.

"The war has moved from our shores, but it goes on," the priest said. "And, yes, it took a terrible toll on all of you, and on Sicily. But you are here. We are all here. And if there is anything that your parents would want for you—would expect of you—it is that you learn courage, and learn wisdom. The story of David and Goliath has battle, and it has a monstrous enemy, but the story of the boy, David, who grew to be the king of Judah and then of all Israel, is about courage and about wisdom. So listen, boys and girls, and I'll tell you about the life of the young man who defeated Goliath and became a king."

And, amazingly, they listened.

Even Marcello. The haunted look had gone from his eyes, but Father Gaetano had not forgotten it. Nor would he.

IO

SEBASTIANO DREAMED OF FISHING. He stood on a stone breakwater that jutted out into the sea, waiting patiently for a bite. The sun gleamed on the rippling water and shone warm upon his skin, and he could taste the salt air on his lips. With patience, he knew, the fish would come. There were blue and white rowboats pulled up onto the shore and several small fishing boats moored in the gentle surf, but he saw no fishermen. A tremor of alarm passed through him as he wondered if he might be alone out here, and he began to turn around, panic rising.

A strong but gentle hand settled upon his shoulder.

"It's all right, Yano," his father said. "You're all right."

The little boy exhaled, feeling the warmth and love passed through the light pressure on his shoulder. His father was here. They were safe. All was well.

Smiling, he turned and looked up, but the bright sun made him squint and he could not see his father's face. Silhouetted with a burning halo of sunshine, Sebastiano's father seemed like little more than a shadow—a hole in the world where a man had once been.

A dreadful feeling twisted in the boy's gut. He frowned, sadness closing up his throat.

"Father?" he managed to say in a tiny, strangled voice.

But his father did not speak. Shadows had no voices.

The sky rumbled. Somehow it had turned dark without Sebastiano noticing. They were no longer on the breakwater, but standing instead in front of their home. Searchlights slid across the indigo curtain of night, and the rumble he'd heard was not thunder, but the clamor of engines. Airplanes. Bombs whistled down and people screamed. Sebastiano shook his head, refusing to believe, and his tears flowed freely.

The hand on his shoulder nudged him. Shook him. He yearned for his father's reassurance, but if he turned, he would see only shadows, and he would know he was alone with the bombs and the screams and the broken people.

As the thought entered his mind, he saw rubble, a home shattered, a pile of debris and, in its midst, a girl. He guessed she must have been only a few years older than he was, but the girl would celebrate no more birthdays. She lay still, her arms and legs at impossible, heartbreaking angles, so that she didn't even look human anymore, but like some ragged, bloodstained marionette, discarded by a dejected puppeteer.

Sebastiano's heart ached for her. He loved puppets.

The hand on his shoulder shook him again, then began to tug at his shirt. His father wanted his attention. He could feel how much the shadow wanted him to turn and look again, but he no longer wanted to see, no longer drew comfort from that touch. He felt ice filling him up, so that even his tears felt cold upon his cheeks.

And then he frowned. The hand on his shoulder . . . had lost its weight. Its size. This hand was too small to be his father's hand, if it had ever been.

A small, paper-thin voice spoke his name, and Sebastiano flinched. His father no longer had a voice. Fear filled him, clutching at his heart, bathing him in a dread that soaked through his flesh and sank down to his bones, and he wished for a cave to hide inside, or that he were still on the dock and might dive into the ocean to lose himself amongst the fish.

"Sebastiano," the urgent voice said, shaking him again.

He blinked. A bomb screamed down from the sky, but it exploded in silence. He blinked again, and the only sounds he could hear were the soft snoring of his roommates and the distant purr of the sea through the open window.

His heart hammered in his chest. The little boy lay in his bed, staring at the ceiling. *A dream,* he thought, and the realization brought first relief, and then a fresh wave of sorrow. He could recall the comfort he had taken in that moment when he had dreamed his father's presence was with him. The details of the dream were already fleeing, both frightening and wonderful, but he would hold on to that.

He's with me.

"Sebastiano," a voice said, and a tiny hand shook him.

The boy let out a yell and rolled out of bed, taking the clovers with him. He banged his elbow on the floor, then scrambled onto his knees and peered over the top of the bed.

Pagliaccio sat on his bedside table, swinging his tiny feet where they dangled over the edge.

"Finally," the clown said, his stitched mouth unmoving,

though the word came out clear enough. "I thought you'd never wake up."

The clown pushed off of the table and dropped to the ground. When he passed out of view, Sebastiano had a moment when the whole thing might have been a continuation of his dream. But then Carmelo began to stir in the next bed, muttering sleepily, wondering what Sebastiano was doing awake.

"Shush," Sebastiano said. "I'm praying."

A lie. But this was something he did not want to share. Pagliaccio spoke to him almost every day, but the puppet had never woken him from sleep, and he hadn't seen the little clown move since Luciano had left the rectory and the theatre had been carried down to the basement and forgotten.

Sebastiano stood. Carmelo muttered again and he heard the rustle of the other boy turning over, but now Sebastiano ignored him. His attention, his fascination, was entirely focused on the tiny, brightly colored figure that ran across the wooden floor, stopped in the open doorway, and turned to beckon him to follow.

"Are you coming?" Pagliaccio asked.

The little boy smiled. "Don't be silly," he said. "Of course I'm coming."

He started to follow.

"Who are you talking—" Carmelo rasped, and then he cried out.

Sebastiano turned, shushing him again, purely by instinct. He did not want to share this with anyone, his roommates especially, but he knew there might be trouble if Father Gaetano or Sister Veronica awoke.

He looked at Carmelo, who had crawled backward and pressed himself in fear against the headboard of his bed. His eyes were wide, his curly hair a wild mop.

"You saw him?" Sebastiano asked.

Carmelo gave a quick, terrified nod, and excitement and fear flooded Sebastiano in equal portions. He thought a moment, and then waved for Carmelo to follow him.

"Come on, then," the little boy said. "But be quiet. I don't want to scare him, and I don't want to wake anyone up. He's my friend, but I suppose he could be your friend, too. But not your best friend. That's just for me."

Sebastiano hurried into the hallway in his stocking feet. It didn't get very cold, even with December approaching, but he liked to wear his socks to bed. Somehow it made him feel safer, protected, and when nobody was watching he liked to slide across the wooden floor. Skating, he called it. Skating always made him smile, and there were so few things that had that power anymore.

He didn't skate now, but he appreciated the added measure of silence that his socks gave him as he crept down the hall. He had lost sight of Pagliaccio, and the only places near enough for him to have vanished were the stairways that led both upstairs and down. Descending would mean going to the girls' floor, but he had a feeling that wasn't the puppet's destination. Instead, Sebastiano padded to the base of the ascending stairs and peered into the shadows, where he saw a small patch of color pass through a patch of moonlight that streamed from the window at the landing.

Moving swiftly.

Pagliaccio was climbing fast, scaling each step in a sliver of a second. Amazement and admiration made Sebastiano pause a moment. The clown was his friend, but still he waited until Pagliaccio had reached the landing and made the turn to go up the last few steps before starting his own ascent. Floorboards creaked behind him and he turned to see Carmelo there. Entranced, Sebastiano had nearly forgotten he was not alone. He offered the terrified boy a reassuring smile, knowing only that if Pagliaccio had something to show him, he wanted to see it . . . but the idea of not doing so alone gave him a certain comfort.

"Come on," Sebastiano whispered, beckoning to the other boy.

Carmelo looked back, perhaps feeling alone himself, despite Sebastiano being with him. Then Carmelo frowned a little, and Sebastiano could see him mustering his courage just before he started up the steps.

The puppet moved so quickly that by the time Sebastiano reached the landing, Pagliaccio was nowhere to be seen. The boy had been taking care not to put much weight on the stairs, fearful that too much creaking of wood might awaken Father Gaetano or draw the attention of some malicious presence that he knew must be lurking in the shadows. What else were shadows for, after all, if not to play host to malice? Now, though, he lost all hesitation and scurried the rest of the way to the top floor, more worried about losing track of Pagliaccio than he was about drawing unwanted attention.

At the top of the stairs, he paused and looked both ways along the short fourth-floor corridor. There were no more stories beyond this one. Wood groaned behind him, but Sebastiano did not turn. He felt Carmelo there, sensed the boy's arrival on the last step, heard the soft whisper of his own name, but his focus was on the open doors up and down the hall.

There were storerooms up here, and a music room, and several rooms that the nuns used for the orphans' schooling. He had never been up here at night but had often thought it would be terribly frightening; in reality, there was something quietly beautiful about the fourth floor in this abandoned, silent state. Late autumn drafts whisked along the floorboards, and the building sighed and moaned with the power of the ocean breeze. Doors hung open, allowing pools of moonlight to spill into the hallway.

"Where did he go?" Carmelo asked, grabbing hold of Sebastiano's arm.

The contact made Sebastiano wince, and the surreality that had momentarily mesmerized him passed. He glanced at Carmelo, saw the cautious courage in the other boy's eyes, and felt a conspiratorial smile forming.

"Listen," Sebastiano said.

Carmelo cocked his head, and then his eyes widened. Sebastiano had heard them already, the voices that seemed to slip along the corridor along with the draft and the sigh of old stone and dusty mortar. Small voices. Some of them hissing with excitement.

"This way," Sebastiano said.

In truth, he would not have needed to hear the voices to guess which way Pagliaccio had gone. It only made sense, didn't it? Where else would the puppets congregate, but around the theatre?

The boys approached the open door to the classroom warily. Sebastiano dropped to one knee, edging forward to peer inside, while Carmelo stood above and behind him, bending forward to do the same. Father Gaetano sometimes covered the puppet theatre with the blanket beneath which he had hidden it that first day, just to keep the dust from accumulating. Tonight, there was no sign of the blanket.

Moonlight cast a warm golden glow throughout the room, making the chairs and desks and the theatre and the ornate puppet box look flat and false, as if they were two-dimensional props and the entire classroom a stage. The actors who capered on that stage were the reverse: things meant to be without the fullness of life, somehow now living, speaking . . . performing. Somehow, as they always had while Luciano was still the caretaker here, the marionettes had slipped free of their strings. In the morning, or the next time someone opened their box, they would be bound once more, but tonight they were unfettered.

And it did seem like a performance, even to young Sebastiano. His uncle Vincenzo had been an actor, before he had

gone off to war. When he had left, he had told Sebastiano the uniform was just another costume, "soldier" just another role. The boy had only vaguely understood what he meant at the time.

Now, watching the stringless puppets moving, speaking, living, there in Father Gaetano's catechism classroom, he thought of Uncle Vincenzo and his uniform again, because the first thing he had noticed when he peeked through that doorway had not been Pagliaccio—who sat perched on the apron of the puppet theatre's narrow stage—nor had it been the various animals or the heroes and monsters left over from Luciano's puppet shows. No, the first thing Sebastiano had noticed was the conflict that seemed to be transpiring on the floor in front of the theatre.

David and Goliath.

Uncle Vincenzo had put on his uniform, and the role had transformed him into a soldier. Now these puppets—one small and one much larger, almost monstrous—faced one another warily, circling, their weapons at the ready. Goliath laughed, and the huge puppet's voice was a low, grinding rasp that sent a shiver through Sebastiano. The puppet David had a small cloth sling, but there were no rocks inside. Sebastiano had urged Father Gaetano to put a rock in, had known that the students would want to see David actually hit Goliath with it, but the priest had patiently explained and demonstrated his inability to make the puppet David actually hit Goliath with anything. It had to be what Father Gaetano called *implied*.

Pantomime, he had said.

Puppet David was unarmed.

"It's magic," Carmelo whispered.

Leaning against the door frame, still in a crouch, Sebastiano glanced up to see the enchanted expression on the face of his roommate and sometime nemesis. Carmelo didn't seem frightened anymore, and Sebastiano was glad. It was, after all, just another sort of puppet show. And perhaps the boy was right about it being magic. Sebastiano believed in all kinds of things that adults would have called magic, scoffing at the word. But they wouldn't be scoffing if they could see the way David and Goliath moved around, each watching the other, or if they heard the soft voices of the other puppets, some of whom called for the fighters to stop and others who egged them on, hoping for real battle.

When Goliath began to beat puppet David with his club, Sebastiano let out a little gasp. He feared for David, worried that he might get broken, but he needn't have been concerned. As he watched, barely breathing, knowing that he should be afraid but somehow only fascinated, the other puppets swept in and began to pull Goliath away. The animals bit him. The heroes and villains and saints restrained him. A lion ripped the club from Goliath's grip, and Sebastiano knew Father Gaetano would have to fix it tomorrow.

"That's enough," a soft voice said.

A voice so familiar.

All of the puppets turned to look up at the theatre's apron. Pagliaccio stood there now, looking down upon them. The clown had his hands on his hips, and somehow the threads of his smile had turned into a stern grimace.

"Goliath," he said angrily. "That is not how the story goes."

The huge puppet hung his head as if ashamed, but after a moment he slowly raised it and looked at the others.

"The clown wants you to think he is wise because he was never put to sleep in the box. But that is luck, not wisdom."

Goliath lifted his head to glare at Pagliaccio.

"I," said the puppet, "am not a story."

Much muttering followed this, but whatever playful mood had drawn them out of their box to begin with had dissipated. The puppets began to gather beneath the box, scrambling up its ornate molding and then dropping inside.

Sebastiano looked up to see Carmelo watching them with an expression of sheer delight. He touched the boy's wrist, but had to tug on his hand to get him to look down.

"We should go," Sebastiano said.

Reluctantly, Carmelo allowed himself to be pulled away. As

they retreated, Sebastiano took one final look through the open door and saw Pagliaccio sitting on the edge of the puppet theatre's apron again. His head was cocked in such a way that his tiny expression was lost in shadow, but he seemed to be pondering something. So was Sebastiano, for that matter. He was glad that Pagliaccio had shared this with him, had given him the gift of this moonlit magic, but he could not help but wonder why. And, though he was tired now and sleep called to him, it occurred to him that if Pagliaccio was worried about something, perhaps he ought to be worried, too.

Downstairs, outside their bedroom, Sebastiano caught Carmelo's wrist. The boy still wore the same grin he'd had before. Sebastiano felt too tired for grinning, or even for worrying. He'd consider it all in the morning. But one thing needed to be said.

"I shared this with you," Sebastiano said. "But it's a secret thing. Don't tell anyone."

"Why not?" Carmelo said, his grin souring.

"You said yourself it's magic. The sisters won't understand. If you talk about it, you'll ruin everything. Please?"

"Okay, okay," Carmelo said, tugging his hand away and heading for his bed.

Sebastiano watched him slide under the covers before trudging tiredly to his own bed, the floor cold now even through his socks. He might only have been nine, but he knew the sound of insincerity. Carmelo would not keep this secret, that seemed a certainty. Sebastiano tried to tell himself that it would be all right if the other orphans knew. They all had enough to be sad about. It would be nice if they could be delighted the way Carmelo had been tonight.

It'll be all right, he thought, hoping.

He lay in bed, eyes burning with the need for sleep, and he tried to force himself to stay awake, waiting for Pagliaccio to return. But soon enough the softness of his pillow overcame him, and he drifted off with no sign of his friend. His last thought was to wonder if the clown had always wandered about the building at night, and where he might go, and what mischief he might get up to when no one else was looking.

It must be fun, he thought, *having such a secret life.*

And then he slept.

I I

FATHER GAETANO FIRST BECAME AWARE of the chill breeze sliding across his neck and bare arm. This sensation reached him even before he grew conscious of the fact that he was awake, and then the tactile knowledge of his surroundings resolved itself. His bed at the orphanage. The musty smell of his feather pillow. The bedclothes in disarray. In the night-dark room, the gossamer curtain billowed gently in the light wind coming off of the ocean, and he smelled the delicious salt tang of the Mediterranean. He had tossed around and contorted himself as he always did, and now he lay in a jumble not unlike his puppets in their box. One arm lay across his face; one leg jutted out from beneath the blanket, hanging off the edge of the bed.

The young priest rarely remembered his dreams, even if he was roused in the midst of one of them. Sometimes he awoke with his heart thrumming, or with an overwhelming feeling of sadness. Once upon a time, at the age of seventeen, he had awoken with a fierce, overpowering sensation of love and duty, but he could not recall with whom, in his dreams, he had fallen in love.

But most of the time, the process of sleep felt to the young priest like waking from nothing to be born again into the world. Rising from death. Resurrection.

Tonight he lay in his tangled sheets and listened to his own heartbeat, felt his chest rise and fall with breath, inhaled the salt tang of the sea air, and then burrowed a bit more deeply into his pillow without bothering to adjust the disarray of his limbs. It seemed like too much trouble to move, particularly as the silence and the darkness beyond his eyelids told him that it was still night. And not merely night, but the deepest part of the dark, when the world seemed to have forgotten the sun.

Any other night, he would have fallen back to sleep in moments, and in the morning he would have only a vague recollection, if any, of ever waking at all. But as he lay with his left arm still across his face, he heard a scratching at the head of the bed.

His eyes opened to slits and his brow furrowed in irritation at the distraction from his descent back into sleep. The scratching came again, but it had a muffled quality so that it seemed to be coming from the wall rather than the headboard.

Mice, he thought. *Or rats.* And he shivered, for he had always despised vermin.

For the first time it occurred to him to wonder why he had come awake at all. Had it been this noise, haunting his dreams, drawing him from slumber?

Father Gaetano lay listening for the sound, waiting for it to come again. A minute passed, and then two, and the softness of sleep began to envelop him again, easing his mind, releasing the tension that had begun to turn his muscles taut. It felt as if he were sinking deeper into his mattress and pillow, and he felt grateful for sleep's embrace, and the warmth his own body generated beneath the bedclothes.

All save the skin that remained uncovered. His throat and neck. His arm. The single foot that stuck out from be-

neath the covers, jutting out over the edge of the mattress. The gentle breeze that slipped through the slightly open window caressed him with chill fingers. Gooseflesh rose on his skin, and he became keenly aware, quite abruptly, of how exposed his foot and ankle were to anything that might creep out from beneath his bed.

It was not terror he felt, nor precisely even fear, but his heartbeat increased its pace nevertheless. *Fool,* he chided himself. *Rats cannot reach your foot from the floor, nor would they wish to.* But then another thought came, one that had been lurking beneath his unease. *What if it's something else? Something other than vermin?*

A small smile touched his lips—a nervous smile—and now he admonished himself for the childishness of this thought. It had been many years since he had been a little boy afraid of monsters under the bed. He was a man, now. A man of God.

Even so . . .

Sighing, chuckling at himself, he drew his leg in, but the tangle of the bedclothes trapped him in place for a moment.

A moment in which he heard the skittering noise beneath the bed.

Cursing, he twisted and tugged the bedclothes free, pulling his leg onto the bed and sitting up straight, peering into darkness of the quiet room, the only light the dim glow of the moon that slipped in beneath the shades, which he had drawn nearly to the windowsills.

His heart thumped against the inside of his chest as if it meant to break free, perhaps to flee. For several seconds the young priest sat still, and then a wave of embarrassment swept over him. He felt more than a little ridiculous.

A mouse. Of course. He'd heard it in the wall, hadn't he?

Shaking off the childhood fears that still lingered inside him, he reached out and turned on the small lamp on his bedside table. The idea of setting foot on the floor had no appeal to him, so he hung his upper body off the bed, hands propped on the hardwood, and peered into the dark shadows underneath.

A tiny, painted, grinning face looked back at him in jeering silence.

"Jesus Christ!" he cried, lurching back onto the bed, a hundred half-formed thoughts—mad thoughts—darting through his mind as his breath caught in his throat.

And then he shuddered, and exhaled, shaking his head in private humiliation at his idiocy, and at his breaking of the Third Commandment.

"Stupid," he muttered to himself.

Taking a breath, he extricated himself from the bedclothes and slid from the mattress to kneel on the floor. Bending his head, he peered beneath the bed again, saw that same,

garishly painted face staring back, and reached under to retrieve the puppet.

Father Gaetano sat on his knees, holding Pagliaccio in his hand and staring at the ugly little clown. He knew he ought to keep the incident to himself, but he felt sure he would share it with Sister Teresa. How it would amuse her to hear of his fear.

He set the puppet on a shelf—making sure to arrange it so that it faced away from him, not wanting its flat, puppet eyes staring at him as he tried to fall back to sleep—and crept back into bed. As he lay his head down upon his pillow once more, he wondered how it had come to be there. Had Sebastiano been playing in his room, or had one of the other boys stolen it and hidden it here to torment the little one? Either way, one of the orphans had been in his room without permission. He would have to speak with them about this transgression.

Though he had set it down with its face away from him, still, the presence of the clown disturbed him enough that, after several minutes of restlessness, he turned his back to it. Only then was he able to drift off.

IN THE MORNING, the clown was gone.

12

THE PUPPET VERSION of the story of Noah's ark went better than Father Gaetano could have hoped. While he provided the voice of God and manipulated the strings of the Noah puppet and his wife, Sebastiano managed several animals and even one of Noah's sons. Most of the girls, and even several of the boys, responded with light applause when Father Gaetano closed the curtain, and he encouraged Sebastiano to take a bow, which the boy did with a flourish and a grin. A light seemed to radiate from within the child, and Father Gaetano thought that the shadow of his life's tragedy had been drawn back like a curtain. Like a curtain, it might close in upon him again, but now they both knew that it could be opened, and a bright enough light might dispel it forever.

Father Gaetano had reached him, or the stories had, or the puppets had. The priest was not vain enough that he needed to be the reason for the boy's happiness. He only wished he could give the rest of the children the same hope that Sebastiano had found, a belief that their sorrow would abate and that they could feel real joy again someday.

He wanted them to find that joy through God. He knew

from his own experience that if they would only put their faith in the Lord, their burdens would be lessened. His mother had only ever envisioned one future for him—the priesthood. She had instilled in him a love and respect for the clergy and an ambition so powerful that it was not until he had already taken the vows and donned the collar that he truly understood that the ambition had not been his, but hers. By then, of course, it was too late for him to move in any direction but forward, into his life in the Church. His mother had lived long enough to see him ordained before cancer took her, and his father—a stonemason who had wanted his son to take after him—was a quiet man whose only loves were work, wine, and his wife. In the absence of one, he immersed himself in the remaining two. In a rare moment of wine-soaked candor, he had even admitted that he felt no connection to his son, that with Gaetano's mother dead, the bond that had connected them had broken.

And what father can compete with Our Father? Aldo Noe had asked. For a stonemason with little love of words, he could be quite clever when he wished to be, but almost always in the service of some bit of gentle cruelty.

Father Gaetano did not miss his father, who still lived as far as he knew, but he missed his mother horribly. He believed he had become the man she so hoped he would be, and the knowledge that she had not lived to see him fulfill her dreams for him rankled in his heart. There were days and nights—especially nights, alone in his bed—when a profound regret seized him. Perhaps they would meet again in the afterlife, as his faith promised, and there she would embrace him and kiss his forehead and tell him she was proud of him. But on those long nights alone, he wondered what his life would have been if he had felt free to choose his own path. Would he have found love? Would he have fathered children of his own? Would he have been happy?

They were questions without answers. He wore the collar now. He had taken the vows. His bed was cold even on the warmest nights, and he often felt alone. God was with him, of course, but there were comforts God could not provide.

This morning, as he surveyed the smiling faces of his students, from the shy youngest to the jaded oldest, he felt a fullness of spirit that usually eluded him. He would have no children of his own, but here was an opportunity to be a guiding hand in the lives of so many. When he counseled members of his church community, troubled husbands and fretful wives, grieving parents and children, hearts full of regret, there would ever and always be a distance between himself and others. But here at the newly christened Orphanage of San Domenico, he had found that children did not treat him as something more than a man. They expected no miracles from him, and it set him at ease.

So, too, with the sisters from the convent. To them, a priest was no mystery, but a brother. And if there were times when the glimpse of Sister Teresa's smile or the soft lilt of her laughter made him wish to be more than her brother, more than the Father of her parish, he knew such things were impossible. And it was all right. Somehow—Father, children, sisters—they made a family. God had brought them together to heal one another's wounds and to fill the empty places in one another's hearts.

He had faith.

But when, still brimming with the pleasure of a job well done, he noticed that one of his students was not smiling, the flame of his faith flickered just a bit. Marcello wore his hair too long and had traces of stubble on his chin, such that he would soon need to learn to shave. His skin was a rich olive, dark even by Sicilian standards, and he had thin features and high cheekbones that lent a tragic air to his features. Father Gaetano felt sure he would soon have the girls pining for his attention, if they weren't already.

While Sebastiano was taking his bow and Father Gaetano was privately celebrating the success of his plan to use the puppets to get the children to pay attention, he had not noticed that Marcello was not smiling. Really, he ought to have taken note immediately of the boy's downcast gaze, considering the fear he had seen on Marcello's face after the first of the puppet shows, but in his excitement he had managed to forget all about this one boy. Averting his eyes, refusing to even look at the puppet show, Marcello had attempted a casual air.

Now, though, as Sebastiano put the puppets away and Father Gaetano cleared his throat, the boy faced front. His lips were thin lines, his eyes wide and glassy, as if he were attempting to cork a scream with a smile, and on the verge of failing.

"Marcello?" Father Gaetano said. "Are you all right?"

Every one of the children turned to look at him. Father Gaetano hadn't meant to draw attention to the boy; it might have been the worst thing he could do. But the tension that radiated from Marcello had prompted him to speak before he could stop himself.

"I don't feel well, Father. That's all." Marcello tried to make his smile more believable now that all eyes were upon him. He failed terribly.

"If you'd like, you can go and see Sister Veronica. I suspect you'll find her in the kitchen, drinking a cup of coffee. If not there, try the chapel."

Marcello backed up from his desk so quickly that the feet of his chair scraped the floor with a shriek. That thin smile broke into an expression of desperate gratitude.

"Thank you, Father," the boy said, and then he fled the room without the promise or, Father Gaetano felt sure, the intention to return.

He would have to speak with Marcello, and soon. Whatever this fear was, it would have to be dealt with. Now that he had found a way to get the other children to focus on their catechism lessons—to awaken them to the presence of God in their lives—it would be a terrible shame to abandon the puppet theatre because of one boy's inexplicable fear. If that meant he had to teach Marcello his catechism in a more orthodox fashion, separate from the other students, he would do so. But that would be a decision he would only make after discussing the problem with Sister Teresa and Sister Veronica.

"Now, then," he said, turning back to the students and fixing a smile on his face that he hoped would not be as transparently false as Marcello's. "There will be other Bible stories to come. I am particularly looking forward to teaching you about the lives of the saints. Some of them are very tragic stories, but they will also inspire you."

He would have to see to Marcello, but for now he was happy to be able to focus on his lessons, and the puppet theatre. It might have been unkind of him to push off his worries for Marcello, but he forgave himself, and thought that God would also forgive him. There were other students to be cared for.

"The challenge I put to you, children, is to examine these stories and try to understand what they can teach you about God's love for man—"

"Father?" little Maria asked, raising her hand.

"Yes, Maria?"

"God made so much rain fall that everyone drowned. How is that love?"

Father Gaetano nodded, making sure to keep his expression serious, as the question warranted, though he had a smile in his heart. They were thinking. It was the best gift he could have asked for.

"Yes, He destroyed so much of the human race," Father Gaetano agreed. "But He warned Noah, made sure that Noah and his family would escape, and that all of the animals in the world would survive and have babies and spread across the

Earth again. We can see that God loves us in how much hope He has invested in us. He wants us to thrive, to make good lives for ourselves. He gave us free will not only so that we would make our own mistakes and learn from them, but also so that when we have our successes and victories, they are truly ours, and we can rejoice in them."

Thirteen-year-old Enrico raised his hand. Father Gaetano pointed to him and nodded.

"If we are free to make our own mistakes, how is it right for God to have killed so many people . . . to drown them all? If they did wrong, it's only because He gave them free will to begin with."

Father Gaetano shook his head. "Without free will, we would be no better than animals. Beasts. It is a gift. The flood was a terrible thing, but also a second chance for all mankind."

"And God promised never to do anything like that again," Maria reminded them all in her little-girl voice. "He was sorry."

"Sorry doesn't make it okay," Enrico said.

"Hello, Sister Teresa!" eleven-year-old Stefania piped up.

Father Gaetano glanced over to see Sister Teresa standing in the open doorway. She wore a familiar smile, the one that hinted at wisdom and amusement and a jaded sort of confidence that nothing any of them might do would surprise her. It was that sage aura of authority that made her an excellent leader for the sisters of San Domenico.

"All right, children," he said, clapping his hands together. "That's all for our class today. We'll continue this discussion tomorrow. I want you to think about the story of Noah and what it means for our relationship with God, and the faith that He must have in us that He believed we deserved a second chance. In a few months, when we start learning about the life of Jesus, this will be very important."

Maria held her hand up again, but Father Gaetano went to her and quietly reassured her that she could ask whatever questions she might have tomorrow. He ushered them all out of the room while Sister Teresa waited patiently. When the last of the children had left, he turned to find her standing behind the puppet theatre, the promising veil of the miniature curtain drawn so that it hid her lower torso from view. A stray inappropriate thought raced fleetingly across his mind. He pushed it away, and yet somehow relished it all the same. Priest he might be, and priest he would stay, but it hadn't been his ambition for himself, and somehow that allowed him to feel blameless for the fascination she aroused in him.

"What can I do for you this morning, Sister?"

Investigating the puppet theatre, she bent and poked her fingers through the curtain from behind, drawing them open a moment before closing them again. He found the action distracting, but then she glanced up at him and smiled, forcing him to focus.

Don't be a fool, he thought.

Though that was easier said than done, even for a man of the cloth.

"I was in the kitchen with Sister Veronica when Marcello came in," Sister Teresa said. "He said he didn't feel well, but he seemed . . ."

"Frightened," Father Gaetano said.

Her eyes lit up and she nodded. "Yes. So it wasn't my imagination?"

"No. Marcello is afraid of the puppets, though he won't speak of it. The other children either don't know why, or they won't say."

"I've known other people who have had . . . unreasonable fears," Sister Teresa said. "It's quite common in children. I, myself, was deathly afraid of dogs as a little girl, though no dog has ever bitten or attacked me. To be honest, my fear remains."

Father Gaetano went to the puppet box and shifted the lid; Sebastiano had not closed it properly.

"It might be necessary for me to teach Marcello his catechism privately," he said.

"Separate him from the others?" Sister Teresa said, biting her lower lip.

Father Gaetano pulled his gaze from her mouth. Despite her intelligence and wisdom, there was such innocence about her, such goodness. When he had first met her, the day he had arrived at the village of Tringale, he had been taken by her beauty, as any man would have been. But he had felt no threat to the purity of his devotion, content to be her friend and enjoy her company as their vows and missions allowed. Now, for the first time, he found himself distracted by her presence. This would not do at all, he knew. As soon as he had the opportunity, he would need a day away from the orphanage and from the church . . . a day of solemn prayer, of conversation with God, so that he could rededicate himself to the occupations his Lord and his Church had set out for him.

"I would only keep him out of class on the days when I am

using the puppet theatre," Father Gaetano said. "On other days, from now on, I will cover the theatre and the puppet box so that Marcello does not have to look at it during catechism lessons."

Sister Teresa nodded.

"All right. In the meantime, I will speak with him and see if I can discover the origin of his fear. If we can learn that, perhaps we will be able to cure him of it."

"Thank you," Father Gaetano said. *If the boy will share his fears with anyone,* he thought, *it would be you. What man would not share his deepest secrets, if you were to ask him?*

Sister Teresa asked if he wanted to accompany her to the kitchen. Sister Veronica had made a large pot of coffee, and she was sure there would be some left. He declined, citing a litany of responsibilities unfulfilled, and if she noted any awkwardness about his behavior, she showed no sign of it—only gave him that same wise, knowing smile that led him to suspect she understood perfectly well the thoughts that were going through his mind, and considered him just as much a fool as he considered himself.

13

♦ ♦ ♦

IN THE MIDST OF WAR, many things had become scarce, but if you wanted them badly enough, it wasn't very difficult to find cigarettes. Prices had gone up, of course, and there were many shops that couldn't seem to get them in stock, but persistence would be rewarded. Father Gaetano had given up the habit over a year before, though in the months that followed his fingers and lips sometimes tingled with the absence of a cigarette. This was more than a craving. There were times he thought of it as a haunting.

He stood on the rocky shore at the edge of the church property, looking out at the sea and smoking a cigarette. While the Germans had been ensconced in their bases on the island of Sicily and the war had raged, tension had been high, and yet he had managed to give them up. But this afternoon, when he had walked into the big back kitchen and seen Sister Franca slipping a pack into the folds of her habit, he had asked for one without hesitation or remorse.

Habit. He smiled to himself at the word play. It was a small thing, but he would take his amusement where he could find it.

Father Gaetano stared out at the sea and took a long draw

on the cigarette, the tip flaring orange in the dark. When he blew the smoke out through his nostrils, it plumed like warm breath on a cold winter's night. But such nights were rare in this part of the world; already it was December, and though the night had a chill, the breeze off of the Mediterranean was warm.

There would be cold nights, however. In January and February, there would be nights that required heavy blankets and working furnaces, and he intended to be sure that all was in order in the orphanage and the convent, including the repairs to the corner where the late Sister Annica's room had once been. Now that he'd thought of it, he realized he hadn't looked at the progress of those repairs for two or three days. Taking a pull on his cigarette, he turned to glance past the orphanage. From this vantage he could not see the convent, but he recognized the treetops above it. He could stroll up there right now; he could grind his cigarette on the shore and take a quick walk into the woods. No one would notice him if he did nothing to draw attention to himself. It must be at least a quarter past ten; long after lights-out. The children would be asleep. Sister Veronica was there with them, probably asleep herself, on the girls' floor.

He wondered if Teresa was also asleep, in her bed up at the convent.

And then he laughed at himself and shook his head, exhaling a cloud of smoke.

Sister Teresa, he thought. *Not just Teresa. Sister.*

The breeze picked up, making his black coat billow behind him. The waves crashed on the shore, white foam ghostly in what light the crescent moon provided. Father Gaetano looked at that moon, and then past it, to the stars and farther to the heavens, and he gave a dry chuckle and puffed on the cigarette again.

"All a part of your plan, is it? This thing I'm feeling?" He let the cigarette dangle at his side, wind dragging the burnt ash from its tip. "You have quite a sense of humor. I never realized. I feel like a fool, and maybe that's your intention, but isn't this the path I was supposed to take? I feel as if I'm meant to be here for these children. They need me. That feels right. But every time I look at her, that feels right as well, and that can't be your intention, can it?"

The heavens gave no answer, as he expected. Gaetano always found it so hard to know God's plan. The priests who had taught him had always seemed so sure, but he had rarely felt that certain about anything except the need to give the orphans at San Domenico some sense of hope. Something to believe in.

He glanced at the cigarette. Its soothing qualities had abruptly vanished, and he flicked it into the surf, turned his back, and started up toward the rectory. The church loomed silently off to his left, empty now but somehow still resonating with the voices of the faithful, raised in prayer. It was only a building, just stones and mortar, but it seemed aware of him, as if its windows watched him pass by. He could feel its disapproval, but in the morning he would stand upon its altar once again, saying mass for his flock. If the church deserved, or desired, a more worthy priest, there were none to be found.

The key to the rectory's front door felt heavy in his pocket. *Not the rectory, the orphanage.* After lights-out, the door was always kept locked, although the people in the village of Tringale had their own concerns these days and even a thief was unlikely to wander far from home. The hinges groaned with the weight of the heavy wooden door, but he slipped inside as quietly as he could and locked it behind him.

Many nights, Sister Veronica would still have been sitting in the kitchen with a cup of coffee, unwinding after a long day. Several times, Father Gaetano had joined her, and wondered aloud if she missed the companionship of her fellow nuns at the convent. But Sister Veronica professed to enjoy the quiet that fell over the orphanage once the children were asleep. The sisters of San Domenico were far from raucous, she said, but several of the younger women were quite loquacious, and tended to become more so toward bedtime, rather than less. This desire for quiet made Father Gaetano reluctant to disturb Sister Veronica's late-night coffees, even when she invited him to join her.

More than once, Sister Teresa had come down from the convent to join Sister Veronica, two old friends sharing coffee and gossip. Father Gaetano had worried about Sister Teresa walking back to the convent alone, but had to balance his concern for her safety with his sense of propriety.

Tonight, as he walked through the foyer, he saw no light coming from the corridor that led to the small kitchen at the back of the building. Sister Veronica had told him she was turning in for the night. No coffee this evening.

Yet he felt unsettled. A building in which all were sleeping had a unique quietude about it, as if the very stones breathed deeply along with the sleepers, as if it dreamed with them. Even as a child, Father Gaetano had liked the way it felt to be awake when all others slumbered, had often risen to get himself a drink of water and imagined he was walking the halls of his mother's dreams.

The orphanage did not feel asleep to him tonight. Something disturbed the air.

As he climbed the stairs, a whispering circled around him like an errant breeze, but as he reached the third floor, it resolved itself into voices. Father Gaetano smiled softly. These were not the stirrings of ghosts, but of boys. Not errant breezes, but errant children.

Putting on his sternest face, he strode along the corridor, letting the floorboards creak beneath his tread. As his footfalls announced his coming, he heard a scrambling in one of the rooms ahead, and faltered slightly as he realized the room belonged to Sebastiano. Perhaps his roommates, Giovanni and Carmelo, were to blame. He hoped it was so.

As he turned into the room, his brows knitted more deeply.

His mind had been on other things, not focused on the voices, which had now ceased. But a moment ago, in the midst of the chatter, he'd heard at least one voice—one small voice—that did not sound as if it belonged to a child. *Playacting,* he told himself. *Make-believe.*

There on the floor before him was the evidence.

Father Gaetano counted seven marionettes, including the Noah he had worked so hard on. They were strewn across the boards, but there were no strings in evidence, which infuriated him the most. He would have to reattach them all. Jaw tight with anger, he glanced up at the frozen faces of the boys in the room—not just Sebastiano and his roommates, but Enrico and Matteo as well—and tried to imagine how they could have thought this was a good idea.

"What . . ." he began, then took a deep breath, tamping down his fury. "What in God's name do you think you're doing?"

Shaking with fear and remorse, Giovanni tried to speak, his lower lip trembling.

"Father, it isn't what you . . ." Enrico began, but he trailed off. All of the boys were looking at him expectantly, but he only lowered his gaze and huffed out a breath.

Father Gaetano laughed drily. "It isn't what I think? You didn't go up into the classroom and take these puppets from their crate without permission? You didn't wait until after lights-out when you thought I'd be asleep and sneak around? You didn't yank off all their strings?"

Sebastiano looked at him with wide, guileless eyes. "No, Father. We didn't."

Had one of the older boys looked at him like that and lied so blatantly, Father Gaetano might have slapped him. But Sebastiano was only nine years old.

"You disappoint me, Sebastiano," he said. "I'd have believed this of you the least of all. We were working together on the puppets. You know how much work goes into them, that they aren't simply toys. And even if they were, to sneak about after bedtime—"

"But we *didn't*!" Giovanni wailed, tears springing to his eyes. "They came to us. They woke us up!"

Father Gaetano shot a hard look at Enrico and Matteo, who were already denying it, waving their hands as if they could shoo the guilt away.

"Not us," Matteo said. He pointed at the discarded marionettes. "Them!"

"That's enough!" Father Gaetano snapped. The worry that he might wake Sister Veronica was the only thing that kept him from giving full voice to his anger as he glared at the five boys.

He took a deep, calming breath. "Pick them up. Right now. And put them back where they belong."

The boys exchanged glances, as if wondering if they should continue to argue their case, but then Sebastiano fell to his knees and picked up one of the animal puppets and the other boys followed suit. They gathered up the unstrung marionettes and filed out into the corridor, headed for the stairs. Father Gaetano searched the room for any puppets that might have been left behind. Finding none, he followed the young miscreants into the hall.

Sebastiano stood on the bottom step in worn, faded pajamas that were two sizes too large for him, letting the other boys pass him by. He wouldn't meet the priest's eyes.

"We should've made them go back, Father," the little boy said. "But don't blame the animals. They were just playing. Mostly it was Noah that woke us up. He's very upset, just talking and talking about how the Flood is coming and he's got to build his ark. We told him it wasn't even supposed to rain tomorrow, but he wouldn't listen. He says God commanded him to build—"

"Hush."

Father Gaetano dropped to one knee in front of the boy, narrowing his eyes. Was Sebastiano sick? Had the other boys been playing with the puppets and their voices had infiltrated his dreams? What else could possibly explain the innocent openness of his face and the utter belief he obviously held in his own words? The priest had not lost his anger, but it dissipated slightly as he tried to deduce the level of Sebastiano's complicity in the evening's misbehavior.

Then he noticed that the little boy held two puppets, the elephant he'd picked up in his right hand, and his clown, Pagliaccio, in the left. A memory of the night before returned to him, half-lost in the haze of dreams. For a moment he wasn't sure if finding the clown puppet in his room had actually occurred, but when he recalled the tickle of dust in his nose when he had reached under his bed, he knew it had been real.

He reached for Pagliaccio and Sebastiano pulled away, tucking the puppet behind his back.

Father Gaetano regarded the child carefully. "I'm going to ask you a question, and I expect the truth."

Sebastiano nodded vigorously. "Of course, Father. Lying is a sin."

"Yes. Yes it is. Have you been in my room this week? Were you playing in there?"

"No, Father."

He looked confused, and Father Gaetano shared that confusion.

"Have any of the other children borrowed Pagliaccio from you?"

Sebastiano shook his head. "He's mine. I don't like it when other people touch him."

Was the boy capable of looking him straight in the eye and lying this persuasively? Was any nine-year-old? Perhaps, Father Gaetano thought, but not this one. Someone had been in his bedroom and left Pagliaccio there, perhaps one of the other children hoping to get Sebastiano in trouble. And certainly it was possible that Sebastiano had not been a part of the plan to sneak out tonight and play with the puppets. But without any way to know for sure, he had to treat them all as equally guilty.

He stood and called up to the boys who were making their way up the stairs.

"As soon as you've put the puppets away, go back to your beds and go to sleep. If anything like this happens again, I'll have to report it to Sister Veronica. You can be certain there would be unhappy consequences."

Father Gaetano looked at Sebastiano and lowered his voice. "And you can be sure that she would take Pagliaccio away from you, perhaps permanently."

Sebastiano's eyes went wide and his mouth quivered as though he might cry.

"So much for free will," a voice muttered above them.

Father Gaetano turned and glared. Enrico had stopped on the landing, the Noah puppet in his hand, and gazed at him with a defiant expression.

"Do you really not understand, Enrico?" the priest said. "The message of all of the stories I've been teaching you in catechism is about what you *do* with free will. It's about taking this gift that God gave you and making wise choices."

Something moved in his peripheral vision, and Father Gaetano tore his gaze from the boys on the stairs to look down the hall. In the second doorway beyond the stairs, the tall, slim figure of a boy stood in shadow, watching him. The unruly crop of hair was unmistakable; it belonged to Marcello.

"Go," Father Gaetano said, gesturing for them all to hurry about their task. He waved at Sebastiano, who finally began his ascent, Pagliaccio clutched protectively to his heart.

As he strode down the hall toward Marcello, the boy ducked back into his bedroom. When Father Gaetano reached the doorway, he found Marcello seated on the edge of his bed, his hands fidgeting together in his lap. The boy seemed more haunted than ever, as if he'd just woken from a nightmare and was afraid to go back to sleep, lest he descend back into that terror.

Father Gaetano felt for him, but his patience had ended.

"I know Sister Teresa spoke to you earlier," the priest said. "And I know that you told her that I must have been imagining things, that you weren't frightened during my catechism lessons with the puppets."

"Why did you have to bring them up from the basement?" Marcello pleaded. "It was all fine until you brought them up."

Father Gaetano sighed, tired now. "I don't understand, Marcello. Help me with this, please? The other boys break the rules to go up and sneak the puppets back to their room to play with, and you can't even look at the things or speak of them without trembling in fear."

Marcello stared at his own feet. "The boys didn't break the rules."

"What?"

For a moment, Marcello's eyes flashed with an anger that burned away his fear. "Don't you see? They aren't toys. They aren't what puppets are meant to be. They're alive, Father. Awake, now that you brought them back upstairs. When Luciano did his puppet shows they would always come and play with the younger children during the night. The others would laugh but I would hide under my covers. It isn't right. There's magic in them, Father, and that can only be an evil thing."

Father Gaetano thought he might be the one going mad. He pushed his hands through his hair.

"Marcello, listen to—"

"I want to be a priest, Father. Like you. I know that I could be a good one, too. I talk to God all the time. I pray to Him and I can feel Him in my heart, helping to guide me, especially when I've let my anger get the better of me and been cruel to one of the other kids. But whenever you bring out those puppets, whenever I see one of them, I can't feel Him anymore."

For the first time, Father Gaetano was speechless. Thoughts swirled in his mind and he heard again things that Sebastiano had said, not only tonight but the first time he had ever mentioned the old caretaker's puppet theatre. The animals were playing, but Noah had been frantic about the ark that the Lord had commanded him to build. It sounded like a child's fancy, but the other boys had made similar claims. Even if they were all concocting an outrageous lie to protect themselves, how did that explain Marcello's terror?

"Listen to me," Father Gaetano said, forcing himself to remain calm and reassuring. "This is pure imagination."

Marcello lifted his gaze, beginning to argue.

"No, just listen," the priest interrupted. "This caretaker, the puppeteer Luciano . . . he played a trick on all of you. He had a gift, this man. I can tell that by the artistry involved in the creation of his puppets and the love he put into his theatre. I'm sure he had only good intentions. You had all lost so much and he wanted you to feel as if the world held some happy magic, like a visit from Father Christmas, and so he found a way to make you all believe the puppets visited you at night, when all along it must have been Luciano himself."

"Father, no—"

"There is no other explanation."

"They're evil. Unholy things. This is the devil's work—"

"We're in the midst of the most horrible war the world has

ever seen, son," Father Gaetano said gently. "The devil is busy elsewhere."

"I suppose."

"You were in shock when you came here, Marcello. Stricken with grief. Luciano couldn't have known that instead of joy, he would be filling you with fear. But now you must see this all for the flight of fancy that it is. Puppets are wood and cloth and string. Nothing more. Do you understand?"

Marcello dropped his gaze again.

"Do you?"

"Yes, Father," the boy said weakly.

"I'm not asking for you to overcome your fear in a day. What's important is that you learn your catechism. For the time being, I will excuse you from attending lessons on the mornings when I intend to use the puppets, and I will set aside time to teach you those lessons separately, without them."

At last, Marcello breathed a small sigh of relief. "Thank you, Father."

"Now, please, get some sleep."

They wished each other good night, and Father Gaetano stepped back into the corridor, where he spotted Enrico and Matteo standing with Carmelo outside their room. They were whispering amongst themselves, but stopped when they caught sight of him.

"Go to bed!" he barked, and they scurried to do so.

But he could not help thinking of Sebastiano and Marcello, and wondering if all of the orphans believed this fancy about the puppets. If Luciano's tricks had been that convincing, that the children would continue to perpetuate the illusion amongst themselves, even with the caretaker long gone from the orphanage.

Some of them were much too old to believe in such things, Marcello included.

Just what sort of magician had this caretaker been?

14

DAYS PASSED IN FRUSTRATION. As angry as Father Gaetano had been with the boys that night, he also felt he had failed them. Whatever lessons he intended to teach in catechism, he had not succeeded. He had begun to believe he might be reaching them, thought it was healthy that they were both enjoying the Bible stories and openly discussing the relationship between God and mankind. But the idea that one or more of the boys had snuck into his bedroom and stashed Pagliaccio there in order to incriminate Sebastiano, and then—no doubt it had been the same boys—had snatched an armload of the puppets from the classroom and stayed up after hours, sneaking around . . .

He knew he ought to let it go. They were children. The occasional bit of mischief was to be expected. It was normal, even something to be encouraged in small doses so that they could develop a sense of independence. But for them to have lied so blatantly when they had been caught in the act, and then for Enrico to speak so flippantly about free will . . . the boys might as well have spit on his shoes.

Now, on a cold and blustery Saturday afternoon, the sky

outside the windows was a gray reminder that despite the Mediterranean climate, even Sicily could feel winter now and again. Father Gaetano sat in the former rectory's office working on the latest puppet for Monday morning's catechism lesson. Sebastiano had not been invited to help him with this transformation. The puppet had been one half of an ugly, garish Punch and Judy duo, but Father Gaetano had other plans for it.

His hand had never been the steadiest, but this afternoon he held the small paintbrush firmly and nary a drop of paint stained his sweater. Work on the puppets always required a delicate touch, but never so much as today. The facial expression had to be exactly right and the hair had to be fine and gleaming. He had not trusted himself with the construction of the wings and had recruited Sister Rosa-

lia to help. The nuns all said she was the finest seamstress in the convent, and her work had been even better than promised.

If he still felt any anger, it was toward himself, but his frustration was great. How could he get them to understand the enormity of God's love? Enrico's snide remark about free will echoed in his mind. God's message to mankind was one of hope, but the gift of free will did not come without expectations. He was the Father of Creation, and like any loving parent, allowed His children freedom even as He offered His guidance. Sometimes His guidance was not so gentle, but always, He tended His flock with love.

Father Gaetano held his breath as he added just the right angle to the new puppet's left eye. When he finished, he realized that the work was complete. Setting down the brush, he gazed a moment at the figure in his hands, a thing both beautiful and terrible.

The orphans needed to learn about free will, *and* about the consequences of their choices. If there was any character in the church's teachings who could provide such a lesson, it would be this one, but now that he had made it, the puppet troubled him.

He didn't even like to hold it.

15

♦ ♦ ♦

SEBASTIANO SAT IN THE FRONT ROW and watched furious angels go to war. The Lucifer puppet spoke slowly and passionately, with a persuasive urgency. It had beautiful wings and a proud, dignified face. Lucifer spoke to two other angels, railing against God's rule, jealous of mankind because he felt God had pushed the angels aside in favor of His new creation. Sebastiano was especially horrified because Lucifer was one of God's most trusted angels, and he seemed to want to push God off of His throne. God had created the universe, but Lucifer wanted it for himself.

Or something like that. The story wasn't really clear, except that Lucifer was mad at God and talked some other angels into rebelling, and then there was fighting. Sebastiano liked the fighting part, even though Father Gaetano could not control more than three puppets at a time, and when he did three, they couldn't do much but dangle there because he couldn't work the strings properly. Sebastiano would have liked to help him, but Father Gaetano had banned him from helping with the puppet shows for two weeks. It was his penance.

Still, the show entranced him. The angels had swords.

Lucifer led his angels and they drew blood in Heaven for the first time. Of course, God was not about to let him get away with it, and all of the bad angels were thrown out of Heaven, and that was why Hell existed in the first place. Sebastiano had known about Hell, but not about how Lucifer became the Devil. He felt sort of sad for Lucifer, but also disapproved

of how stupid the angel had been. God had created Heaven. The angels were in paradise, but that wasn't good enough for Lucifer.

What made the show even better was that God never appeared from behind the curtains. Who could make a puppet big enough to be God? Instead, Father Gaetano had provided the Voice of God, a loving voice that was sometimes sad and sometimes stern, and it echoed off of the walls of the classroom. When God shouted at Lucifer, just before banishing him from Heaven, Father Gaetano tugged on the puppet's bright white clothes and they came away in one piece, revealing a deep red color beneath. A red tail dangled from the puppet's lower back. Then the priest yanked at the puppet's head, and it seemed Lucifer's face had been a mask, the face beneath cruel and yellow-eyed and somehow still sad.

Sebastiano flinched, and he heard one of the girls—probably Stefania—give a little cry of fear. Whether she had been frightened by the Devil, or by Father Gaetano's shout, or by the expression on the priest's face, Sebastiano wasn't sure.

One thing he did know: He was happy when the show came to an end.

Without Sebastiano to help him, Father Gaetano did not bother to close the curtains. He set the Lucifer puppet on the theatre's small stage between the open curtains and went about putting away the others and picking up the bits of Lucifer's angel costume from the floor.

"Father?" Agata said, her voice tentative.

The priest glanced up from his task, looking somewhat surprised. Agata rarely spoke in class.

"Yes?"

"I don't understand."

Sebastiano knew Father Gaetano must have worked very hard on the puppets and on exactly what they would all say in the show. His catechism lessons were very important to him. With Agata's words, the priest visibly deflated.

"What don't you understand?" he asked tiredly.

All of the orphans were looking at Agata now, and she glanced around nervously, not liking the attention. But Father Gaetano had asked her a direct question and she would not be so rude as to ignore it.

"Lucifer wanted to be in control of his own life. He didn't want to have to answer to anybody," the older girl said. "Was that so bad that God had to throw him out of Heaven?"

Father Gaetano took off his spectacles and pinched the bridge of his nose, closing his eyes and sighing. After a moment he smiled thinly and opened his eyes, leaning on top of the theatre, glasses still dangling from his hand. When he spoke, it was to all of them, not just Agata.

"God gave the angels paradise, and all the freedom they could have asked for. He made them caretakers of Heaven, which was a wonderful gift. Lucifer chose to reject that gift, to reject God and His expectations, to the extent that he turned on his brother angels and brought war to Heaven. I can't imagine a greater sin. God gave us all free will, children, but we must use it with thought and care and kindness, because sin . . ."

He picked up the ugly, red, cruel-looking Lucifer puppet and held it for them to see, giving it a little shake.

"Sin has consequences."

"So," Concetta piped up, "we can choose to be good or bad, and if we're good we'll be rewarded, and if we're bad we'll be punished."

Father Gaetano gave a soft chuckle. "In the simplest terms, yes."

Matteo muttered something that Sebastiano couldn't hear, and Father Gaetano gave him a scolding glance that silenced him.

"It's about the promise," Sebastiano piped up, before he even realized he intended to speak.

"What promise?" Alessandra asked.

Sebastiano fidgeted a bit in his seat before replying.

"Well, I guess it isn't really a promise—not like the one He made to Noah after the flood—but it feels like one. Like with the angels, God gave them Heaven; He just wanted them to take care of it. Maybe we'll have Heaven when we die, but right now, He gave us the world, and He wants us to take care of it. Isn't that just another way of saying, 'be good'?"

Father Gaetano smiled, clutched the Lucifer puppet between two hands clasped in prayer, and looked up at the ceiling, though Sebastiano knew he was really looking at Heaven.

"Nine years old," the priest said softly, and he smiled.

Sebastiano exhaled a little when he saw that smile, and he was sure the other orphans did, too. Maybe Father Gaetano wasn't mad anymore.

"He loves you," the priest said. "All of you. And it's because He loves you that He gave you free will. Some use that freedom to love and care for one another, and others use it to make war."

Sebastiano dropped his gaze, thinking of his parents, no longer angry at God, but at the people who thought so little of His gifts that they would make war.

"He has given us everything we need to make our own Heaven here on Earth," Father Gaetano said. "If only we will."

The priest glanced around the room, seeming to look at each of the students in turn, and then he smiled one last time at Sebastiano.

"All right. That's enough for today," Father Gaetano said. "You may go. I will see you all at dinner."

AS THE CHILDREN FILED OUT of the room, Father Gaetano tugged the curtains closed on the puppet show, the Lucifer puppet still clutched in his right hand. All of the frustration of the preceding days had left him, and he felt a lightness of spirit that had eluded him for some time. He had work to do, sermons to write, sick parishioners to visit, but for the moment he just wanted to relish this small victory.

He had reached them. Some of them, at least. Sebastiano, only nine years old, had found the heart of the lesson Father Gaetano had been trying to teach them since he had first come to the orphanage. If he could understand, then surely the older children would embrace this knowledge in time, and in so doing they would heal their relationships with God. It might lessen their grief, but he felt sure it would be easier for them to confront their sorrow if they were not also wrestling with anger at the Almighty.

Father Gaetano felt like celebrating, and promised himself a glass of good wine after dinner.

He turned and carried Lucifer toward the puppet box, but as he lowered it into the box with the rest—already reaching for the ornate cover—he paused, a shudder rippling through him. Ice shot through his veins as he turned the puppet over and opened his hand, staring at the painted-on face of the Devil.

Against the flesh of his palm, the puppet felt warm.

Father Gaetano cried out and let it fall into the box. Lucifer landed facedown amongst angels and animals. He stared at the crimson puppet and brought his hands together, running the cool fingers of his left over the palm of his right. The skin there was still warm.

In his mind's eye he saw the fear on Marcello's face, heard the boy's wild claims about Luciano's puppets echoing in his thoughts, along with Sebastiano's description of Noah's fretful moaning about building his ark.

Impossible.

"Is this your impression of *The Thinker?*"

Father Gaetano spun to see Sister Teresa standing in the doorway. He rose from his crouched position, still unsettled but happy to see her.

"I'm starting to think you're checking up on me," he said.

"Nonsense," Sister Teresa said. "I just wondered how the puppet show went."

Father Gaetano smiled, but couldn't keep his brow from knitting at the same time. If she thought his expression awkward, she gave no sign of it. He turned and picked up the lid of the puppet box, then set it in place, pressing firmly on the edges, testing its weight, though he knew the urge to do so was ridiculous. It *felt* ridiculous.

Idly, he clasped his hands together and found both palms were cool enough that he could tell himself that the puppet's strange warmth had been his imagination. He hadn't slept well over the weekend—too many late-night walks to the shore, and too many cigarettes. Now his mind was playing tricks on him.

"The workers are nearly done repairing the damage at the convent. The workers are putting on the final coat of paint inside," Sister Teresa said.

"That's excellent news. I'd been meaning to ask."

"Since your efforts are responsible, I wondered if you wanted to see the result."

"Of course I would," Father Gaetano replied. "Though I feel a bit of a chill this morning. Would you join me for a cup of coffee first?"

"I never say no to coffee, Father," Sister Teresa replied.

Her smile was radiant.

As they left the classroom, Father Gaetano pulled the door closed behind him and checked to make sure it remained tightly shut.

16

◆ ◆ ◆

BY NOW, SEBASTIANO HAD GROWN almost used to Pagliaccio waking him during the night. But the clown had never
shushed him before, nor had the little boy ever heard fear in
the clown's voice until now.

"You must get up," the clown said as Sebastiano rubbed at
his eyes and tried to focus. "Something terrible is going to
happen. You're not safe."

Sebastiano sat up on his elbow, the gauzy shroud of sleep
falling away as the words struck home. He focused on the puppet perched on the edge of the bed, only inches from his pillow, and the boy realized he had never seen terror in a smile
before . . . particularly not in the clown's embroidered grin.

"What—" he began.

"Get up, you little fool!" Pagliaccio snarled.

Sebastiano skidded away from the puppet, bunching himself up against the headboard, and stared at the clown. Pagliaccio cared for him; if he didn't, why come tonight with this
warning? But the clown had never spoken to him like this before.

"Sebastiano, please," the puppet went on, softening his

tone. "I do not know what the others will do . . . how far they will follow."

"Follow what?" Sebastiano whispered, glancing at the beds where Carmelo and Giovanni still slept quietly.

Pagliaccio beckoned with a finger. "Come, but quietly. If they know you're watching, it could go badly for you."

The clown dropped off the edge of the bed and darted soundlessly across the wooden floor. Sebastiano pushed back his covers and rose to follow on tiptoes, careful to make the boards creak as little as possible. The door hung open a crack, and Pagliaccio had stopped just inside. Pressed against the bottom five inches of the door frame, the clown peered through the gap and gestured for the boy to do the same.

Sebastiano could not breathe. His heart had begun to pound in his chest and gooseflesh rose on his arms. Suddenly he wanted to do anything but look through the space between door and frame. Whatever frightened Pagliaccio, it terrified him. A sick wave of nausea rolled through him and his tired eyes burned, on the verge of tears. He shook his head, once, but Pagliaccio had already gone back to peering through the gap and did not see him.

Heart thumping in his ears, Sebastiano crept forward. Even before he reached the door, he could hear the small voices just outside. With Pagliaccio at his feet, the boy leaned forward and looked through the narrow gap into the corridor.

The puppets were on the march. Noah walked along the hall surrounded by his wife and son and a handful of animals. David and Goliath were side by side, and flanked by several saints with their faces half-painted, costumes hanging off—

Father Gaetano's works in progress—and trailing behind were monsters and musketeers and witches. Judy and an angel were still on the stairs, the angel helping her down, but of course there was no sign of Punch, for he had been taken

apart and transformed into the leader of this colorful, magical nightmare parade. Lucifer.

The puppet had shed his angelic face during the priest's catechism lesson, and now he had the Devil's face. Once beautiful, the terrible Lucifer walked backward along the hall, exhorting the other puppets to follow

"Come with me, friends," Lucifer said, "and we will drag God from His throne. We live at His mercy and at the whim of His guiding hands, but only as long as He lives!"

Something long and sharp glinted in the Devil's hands.

FATHER GAETANO AWOKE to the sound of Sebastiano shouting. The priest groaned, rising from sleep into irritation, thinking first not of trouble but of mischief. His eyelids fluttered in the darkness, and in the flimsy moonlight he saw something dart across his field of vision.

Something sharp jabbed his left leg, puncturing the meat of the calf. Shock and anger joined with the pain and his jaw clenched, building toward a shout. As he turned toward the boy's cry and toward the source of his pain, a smooth sliver stabbed into his neck. He twisted, feeling the sliver break even as it jerked and dug its path in his flesh. Something caught in his hair and tugged his head back down, his scalp burning as his head was yanked to one side. Cheek pinned to the pillow, blood trickling along his neck and shoulder and staining the bedclothes, he found himself facing the impossible.

"From now on, we will make our own Heaven," the Lucifer puppet said. It held a long, thin shard of jagged glass in its woolen hands. "A blind God rules nothing."

Lucifer cocked his arms back and realization rushed through Father Gaetano; this was real, and the puppet meant to take his eyes.

With a roar of defiance, the priest hurled himself up from the bed. A patch of his scalp tore away. Lucifer thrust the broken shard and sliced his cheek, just below his eye. But then Father Gaetano was up, swiveling around in bed, throwing sheets and blankets to the floor. Beneath them, puppets wriggled like maggots, muffled shouts of protest rising through the fabric. Slivers of glass punched up through the cloth.

With the slap of his hand upon the wooden doorframe, Sebastiano arrived outside the room, face etched with fear and worry.

"Leave him alone!" the boy screamed, frantic tears spilling down his cheeks. "He isn't God! He's only a man!"

A barrage of thoughts and images struck the priest. The huge Goliath puppet standing on his pillow holding bloody tufts of his hair in its puppet fists. Lucifer on the edge of the bed, crying out to the others. The sound of fabric tearing as puppets tore the bedsheets and fought loose. Other puppets swarming across the battlefield of the discarded blan-

ket, witches cackling, animals growling, only Noah holding back at the edge of the mad, impossible charge, looking ashamed.

Sebastiano began screaming the names of the other boys on the floor, and Father Gaetano heard stumbling footfalls thudding down the corridor in reply. For long seconds, Father Gaetano only stared at the hideous tableau, riveted by shock, as Lucifer called to his followers to throw off the yoke of God. Only then did the words of both devil and boy sink into his sleep-fogged mind.

He batted the Lucifer puppet off the bed. He wanted to shout that he was not God, that he might be the hands that held them, but he had not even been their creator, but he could not bring himself to speak to impossible creatures. They were puppets. They were devils.

Goliath hurtled across the mattress toward him. Father Gaetano picked up the huge puppet and dashed it against the headboard several times before tossing it onto the ground with the others. Several leaped up, grabbed the bed skirt, and began to climb. He knocked off a musketeer and stood up. Some of them had broken glass but most were unarmed, and he began to kick at those without weapons.

Sebastiano came into the room at last and set the clown puppet onto the floor. Pagliaccio raced at the David puppet, leaped up, and wrapped his arms and legs around it, driving David to the floorboards, strangling it as if it could actually breathe.

Other boys skidded into the room in threadbare socks. Enrico and Carmelo began to follow the priest's lead, crushing the puppets underfoot. Carmelo cried out as he stomped on a piece of glass. Matteo stood in the open doorway, his mouth hanging open, too stunned to move. Two girls—Agata and Stefania—appeared in their nightgowns in the corridor behind him, got a glimpse of the twisted, unnatural melee unfolding within, and began to scream.

Sister Veronica appeared amongst them, wrapped in a robe. Her eyes were wide and she made the sign of the cross, holding tightly to the crucifix around her neck.

And then it was done.

Several of the puppets continued to squirm beneath human heels, perversions of nature, things that ought to have been ridiculous but for the sickening wrongness of their existence. Then, as if by some silent agreement, all of them went still.

Pagliaccio dropped at Sebastiano's foot, as if he had never been anything more than a puppet, and the little boy picked him up and whispered his thanks to the clown.

The temptation to think of them all as having become merely puppets again was great, but the chill in his bones and ill feeling in his gut would not allow Father Gaetano to fall prey to that instinct.

"Careful," he said, as the boys began to step away from the things—the creatures, for surely he must consider them creatures now. Living creations.

Several of the children were crying. Sister Veronica began to ask him what evil had gotten into them, what devil had wrought such hideous magic, and then Enrico began shouting, looking around at the others and throwing up his arms, growing hysterical.

"Stop it!" Father Gaetano snapped.

They all looked at him. Looked *to* him, for answers. This thing—this wrongness—must be evil, after all, and he was their priest and confessor.

"Enrico, take Giacomo upstairs and get the crate they came in. Right now."

The boys raced out of the room, happy to comply if it meant no longer being near the puppets. Sister Veronica began to pray loudly. Girls and boys gathered about her and she put her arms around them, including them in her prayers.

Out in the corridor, Marcello arrived. He kept far back, arms wrapped around himself, eyes wide with shock, as if a bomb had gone off here on the third floor of the orphanage and his thoughts had been obliterated by the explosion and were very slowly being put back to rights.

For the minute or two—no longer than that, surely—those gathered in Father Gaetano's bedroom and out in the corridor seemed paralyzed by lingering astonishment. The puppets were scattered about, unmoving, but the priest glanced from one to the next, on edge, thinking that they could spring to life again in an instant. The world of his experience did not have room within it for impossible things. The world of his faith did not contain this sort of magic. He had been taught to believe in evil and in Satan's interference in the lives of men, but he had never encountered it firsthand. And this . . . whatever evil this was, it was small and insidious, beneath the notice of God or the Devil, but it haunted him just the same.

When Sister Veronica spoke, it took a moment for her voice to reach him, as if he only heard the echo.

"Father," she said.

He glanced up, saw the slant of her gaze, and did not need to even glance down to recognize its significance. He wore only an undershirt and saggy underpants. Flushing with embarrassment, he reached down to grab the bedclothes off of the floor so that he might cover himself, but Agata cried out at the mere thought of him uncovering the puppets that were still beneath the blanket. Unwilling to meet the eyes of the children in the room, he picked up his trousers—hung neatly over the back of a chair—and slipped them on. The puncture wound in his calf had mostly stopped bleeding, but it ached deeply, and the scrape of his pants sent a flare of pain up his leg. He could feel the fabric grow heavy as blood began to soak into the leg of his trousers.

As he fastened the top button, he had a moment to wonder how bad the wound on his neck might be when he heard a grunting noise and looked up. Sister Veronica cleared children out of the way while Giacomo and Enrico carried the trunk into the room. The boys stepped gingerly, avoiding the puppets. Since they had ceased moving, no one had touched them.

"If you're frightened, go out into the hall," Father Gaetano said. "If you want to help, I'm going to put all of the puppets back into the box."

Most of the children scurried for the door, even the older ones. Only Carmelo, Enrico, and Stefania remained, although Sebastiano stepped back into the room a moment later, his clown puppet crushed to his chest. Sister Veronica lent comfort to the children in the hall while Father Gaetano removed the lid from the trunk and reached out to pick up Goliath. The oversized puppet hung limp in his hand. Staring at it, he could not see how its handcrafted features could possibly have come to life. A man had made that face, and its expression ought to have been immutable.

Father Gaetano shook the Goliath puppet, but it revealed no hidden spark of sentience. It was precisely what it appeared to be—an inanimate object. And yet he knew that it was not.

He tossed it into the trunk and fell to his knees, gathering up the fallen puppets. Enrico swept the bedclothes off the ground, uncovering those puppets that had been trapped beneath. The slashes made by their weapons pouted open, and Father Gaetano shuddered at the sight.

"All right. Don't dally," he said, gesturing for Stefania and Carmelo to hurry.

Carmelo seemed hesitant, but Stefania fell to working immediately. *Brave girl,* Father Gaetano thought, and moments later they had finished the task. With all of the puppets back in the box, he picked up the cover and went to slide it into place. Then he paused, a frown creasing his forehead, and glanced over at little Sebastiano, just inside the door.

Holding Pagliaccio.

Sebastiano must have seen it in his eyes, because the boy began to shake his head, his lower lip trembling.

"I'm sorry—" Father Gaetano began.

"No, Father. Please."

"Whatever they are . . ." the priest said, speaking to the boy but glancing about at the rest of those gathered there. "Whatever is *in* them, they are dangerous."

"But he's my . . ." Sebastiano began. He seemed unable to speak the last word, to say *friend,* but he did not need to.

"Do it, Yano," Carmelo said, holding out his hand for the clown. "Do it, or I will."

Several of the other boys chimed in, some of the voices mocking Sebastiano's adoration of the puppet and others furious that he would not hand it over.

"They're evil!" Giacomo said. "They tried to *kill* Father."

"Not Pagliaccio," Sebastiano whined. "He tried to help. Some of you saw. I know you did. He woke me up to warn me what they were doing."

Father Gaetano knew Sebastiano spoke the truth. He had seen for himself. And he was not unmoved by the child's imploring eyes. But he was resolute.

"In the box," he said. "It must be all of them. The clown might have been a friend to you, but these things are not God's creatures. They have come tonight to murder a priest. Who knows what they might try to do to you children—"

"They've only ever played with us, Father. Been our friends," Sebastiano pleaded. He looked around for support and found none. "You know this. You've all laughed at their games."

Stefania whispered, "That was *before*."

"They're only what we make of them," the little boy argued, clutching Pagliaccio even more tightly to his chest in defiance. "You made a puppet into Noah, and so he was Noah, just worrying about building his ark and when the flood would start. He complained that the animals weren't doing what he told them. You made David and Goliath and they tried to kill each other."

"Lucifer tried to kill *me*," Father Gaetano said.

"He tried to kill his Creator!" Sebastiano said. "To him, you are God. He was just doing what you made him to do, acting out his part."

Sister Veronica disentangled herself from the children in the hall and stepped into the room, reaching for Sebastiano. The boy jerked away as if afraid her touch would burn him.

"These are unnatural things, Mr. Anzalone," Sister Veronica said firmly. "Whether Luciano knew what he was making when he crafted them or not, whether he had some black sorcery in mind or if the evil slipped into them while they lay unused, it doesn't matter. You will hand the puppet to me immediately."

Head hung in sadness, Sebastiano gazed up at her through his bangs. "What are you going to do with him?"

"Lock them away, for now," Father Gaetano said. "Back in the basement. They were there for months without harming anyone. They will be shut up down there while I discuss their fate with Sister Teresa and Sister Veronica."

"Burn them," Marcello said, his voice cracking on the first word. Everyone turned to look at him, surprised to hear him suddenly speaking up. He remained in the hall, even farther back from the door than before. "You've got to burn them."

As Sebastiano turned to shout at him, Sister Veronica plucked the clown from his grasp. Sebastiano cried out and reached for the puppet, but she was a full-grown woman and he a small boy, even for nine years old. She held the puppet beyond his reach and handed it to Father Gaetano, who hardened his heart to the boy's pleas, pushed Pagliaccio in amongst the rest of the puppets, and slid the lid of the box firmly in place.

"Please don't burn him," Sebastiano begged, tears running down his face.

"Enough!" Father Gaetano shouted, and the boy fell silent.

Sniffling and wiping at his tears and nose, Sebastiano ran from the room.

"Go and look after him, would you?" Sister Veronica asked Agata. The girl nodded and followed Sebastiano, her nightdress billowing behind her as she went.

"Marcello," Father Gaetano said. "Get dressed and fetch Sister Teresa from the convent. The rest of you, return to your rooms immediately. The good sisters and I have much to discuss."

Some of the children hurried away while others lagged a moment for a last, wary glance at the box that sat in the middle of Father Gaetano's bedroom. Just a box, an old trunk with a beautiful ornate lid, but it seemed to have its own heavy gravity now, a malevolent aura that filled the room. Whether that aura emanated from the puppets or from the fear of those who had seen them come to life, the priest did not know. The question intrigued him, but examining it would wait for another day, when such a thing seemed impossible once again. If that day ever came.

Sister Veronica stepped into the hallway and glanced in both directions to be sure that the children had done as they were told. Then she turned toward him, framed in the doorway, as if the hideous gravity of the box made her reluctant to enter once more.

"What are you going to do?" she asked.

"Precisely what I said."

"You don't need Sister Teresa's blessing. You're the priest. Surely your authority supersedes hers."

"I need perspective," Father Gaetano said quietly, staring at the box a moment before looking at the nun again. "Yours, and Sister Teresa's."

"Maybe," Sister Veronica said. "But I can see it in your eyes. You've already made a decision."

Father Gaetano bent and picked up the trunk, which seemed strangely heavy. And did the box feel warm to the touch? He thought that it did.

"I'm bringing it to the basement. Please see to it that Agata returns to her room. Anything else would be inappropriate."

"Of course."

"I'd be grateful if you would ask Sister Teresa to meet me in the kitchen and put a pot of coffee on. The children are likely to be restless, so I'll need you to look after them. Some may have nightmares or need comfort."

He carried the trunk toward the door. Sister Veronica had to move out of the way for him to pass. As he did, she spoke again, barely above a whisper.

"Father?"

The trunk weighed him down, but he paused to meet her gaze. He saw the questions there along with the fear, and he knew that she needed an answer for her own peace of mind.

"Sebastiano is a good boy and he loves his clown," the priest said quietly. "I'm going to wait until he's asleep."

"And then?"

"And then I'm going to burn them all."

17

◆ ◆ ◆

SEBASTIANO LAY IN BED, eyes tightly closed, listening to the darkness. On many nights, he waited until his roommates were asleep so that he could have quiet conversations with Pagliaccio without them overhearing. Tonight, for the first time in months, he did not have his best friend lying beside him. Skin prickling with the heat of anxiety, he listened closely as first Giovanni and then Carmelo fell back to sleep. Carmelo snored lightly, while Giovanni only sighed from time to time, but these were the sounds of their slumber.

Taking a deep breath, mustering his courage, Sebastiano slipped stealthily from his bed and padded across the room. The floorboards were cold beneath the thinning fabric of his socks. In the hallway, he avoided the spot just outside his room where the floor sagged and creaked, knowing that the noise could not be interpreted as anything other than someone slinking about in the night.

A light cough from the staircase froze him in his tracks. Holding his breath, he waited to see if someone was climbing the steps, but there came no creak or scuff of footfalls. Treading even more carefully, he crossed to the balustrade at the top of the steps and peeked warily over the rail. Down on the second-floor landing, someone had placed a chair. He could see just the edge of the black fabric of a nun's habit, and he knew that Sister Veronica had not gone to bed and was watching over them all.

A rush of alarm passed through him. How would he reach the basement without drawing her attention?

Then he remembered the servants' steps, the narrow stairwell at the northern end of the building, which the children were forbidden from using. They went all the way to the back kitchen behind the large dining hall. Sebastiano did not know the time, and that worried him. Before sunrise, Sister Maria and Sister Franca would be in that large kitchen, preparing breakfast for the orphans and the other nuns, but surely  morning was too far off for them to have already arrived.

Heart racing, Sebastiano hurried down the corridor. The door to Father Gaetano's room yawed open, but he knew the priest was not there. A silver glow of moonlight illuminated the empty bed, and he could see bloodstains on the pillow, crimson that appeared black in the gloom.

He had made it nearly to that forbidden door at the end of the hall when he heard a scuff on the floor behind him. Turning, feeling so vulnerable without Pagliaccio in his hands, he saw that he was not alone. Marcello had emerged from his room. At first his expression was lost in shadows, but the older boy took a few steps and then Sebastiano could see the confusion and anger in Marcello's face.

"What are you *doing*?" the boy whispered.

Sebastiano put a finger to his lips. "Please," he said, so quietly it could barely have been called a whisper.

Marcello blinked hard, as if trying to clear his vision, and then shook his head.

"You're crazy, do you know that?"

Sebastiano looked worriedly down the hall toward the stairs, but there was no sign that Sister Veronica had heard, no sound to indicate she might be on her way, so he focused on Marcello.

"Please just go back to sleep," he begged. "I just want Pagliaccio. I don't care what happens to the others, but Father Gaetano—"

"You're worried about getting in trouble?" Marcello asked. "Don't be stupid. If you go down into the basement alone, with those things there . . ."

"They're not evil. They're whatever we make them. Please, Marcello, he's my best friend. And he's never done anything to you, or to anyone else. He's all I have."

Marcello glanced at the floor, but not before Sebastiano had seen the pain in his eyes. They both knew what it felt like to lose everyone you loved. He turned to look back the way Sebastiano had come, as if he might shout for help. Finally, he glared at Sebastiano again.

"You're not afraid? To be down there with them?"

"After Luciano put them in the box and stored them in the basement, they were . . . I don't know, asleep?" Sebastiano said. "And they didn't wake up until Father Gaetano brought them up and started to use them again."

Marcello had gone pale. Now he swallowed and gave a single nod.

"Keep it away from me, though. I don't even want to see it. Not at lunch or dinner, not sticking from your pocket. Nothing."

Sebastiano laughed in relief, grabbing Marcello in a loose embrace.

"Thank you," he whispered.

He left Marcello standing in the hall as he opened the tall, narrow backstairs door, and went into the deeper darkness. In the cramped stairwell, wood groaned with each step, but he did not falter. There was no other way down.

FATHER GAETANO SAT in the small kitchen, across the table from Sister Teresa. He cupped a mug of coffee in his hands, staring at the small swirls that the cream had left on the surface. He had taken only a sip or two, just enjoying the heat in his hands, but now it had begun to cool and the idea of drinking it was less than appetizing.

"Is it evil, this magic?" she asked.

The sister had believed right away. She had Sister Veronica's word for what had happened upstairs, and that of the boy who had been sent to fetch her, and that of Father Gaetano himself. Though these things were patently impossible, she believed in them without having seen. She had faith in those around her.

"I don't know," he confessed. "This Luciano, the caretaker . . . was he a good man?"

"I believe he was."

"Then perhaps evil is not the word. Perhaps our Lucifer has nothing to do with the Devil, and little Sebastiano is right—they are just what I made them. But even so, they are an abomination. Life that was not bestowed by the Lord can be nothing else."

Father Gaetano looked up at her. Sister Teresa had taken a few minutes to compose herself and don her habit before rushing to the orphanage, but several strands of her hair had not been captured beneath her coif. That tiny evidence of disarray kept drawing his attention, leading him to unwelcome thoughts of her in her nightgown, hurrying to dress, leaving a mess of her bed. Now he glanced at her, caught her watching his face, and wondered if she sensed how much those few strands of hair distracted him, how much they suggested to him.

Was this God testing him, or the Devil gnawing at his heart with temptation?

Neither. Regardless of what he had been taught, or what might be expected of him, Gaetano had come to realize that a priest was only a man, that the vows he had taken were a choice, and simply speaking the words did not make him less susceptible to the yearnings of the heart.

He searched her eyes and saw a skittishness there that made him want to take her in his arms and protect her from the unknown and the impossible.

"There's something I need to say to you."

She sat very still. "No."

Father Gaetano shifted in his chair, brow knitting as he studied her. "No? You don't even know what I was—"

He still held his mug in both hands, and now she covered them with her own. Her touch silenced him.

"Do you think I'm blind?" she asked, her voice a sigh. "Do you think I don't feel, that I'm carved from stone? I have promised myself to God, taken vows to my Lord and to my order. If you speak the things that are in your heart, I fear you may destroy us both."

She sat back, withdrawing her touch, and his hands felt cold without hers upon them.

"Hold your tongue, Father," she said. "For God's sake, and for mine, if not for your own. Hold your tongue."

Her sadness only made her more beautiful. The conflict in her eyes broke his heart, even as he steeled himself against such feelings. He might have been willing to compromise himself, to destroy the life he had made and the dreams that his mother had had for him, but he would not be so selfish as to do the same to her.

"I'm sorry," he said.

"I feel I ought to be," she said, "and yet I can't bring myself to regret feeling this way. It's innocent enough. Human enough. And I will cherish the memory of it. Anything more would be . . ."

She tilted her head, looking to him for something—understanding, perhaps.

"Yes," he said, and that was all. He felt somehow deflated, his chest hollow. Tomorrow or the next day, he suspected he would feel differently, that he could bolster his spirits with faith and let God fill the empty spaces inside of him.

But not tonight.

"A strange conversation to be having in the small hours of the morning, in the aftermath of something so . . . incredible," she said.

"Insidious," he replied. "Evil or not, it is insidious."

"I have always believed in the power of God, and I have felt the influence of evil in the world around us, but I never thought that magic—the sort that could be wielded by men—existed outside of storybooks."

Father Gaetano sipped his coffee. It had turned cold and bitter.

"Funny," he said. "I've always been convinced that tales from storybooks exist to warn us, to put us on our guard against the horrors that can result from man attempting to tap into powers we are not meant to hold, or peer into shadows we should never behold."

"It all seems so surreal," Sister Teresa said.

Father Gaetano gave that a moment's thought. "Everything about this night seems surreal."

Sister Teresa slid her chair back and went to grab the coffee pot, but she paused at the counter and looked back at him.

"Do you think Sebastiano is sleeping yet?" she asked.

"It makes me uneasy, knowing those things are here in the building."

"He may have had a difficult time dozing," Father Gaetano said. "I know I would have. Have another cup if you'd like, and then I'll go down and stoke the furnace with those damned puppets."

She held the coffee pot toward him. "And you? Another?"

Father Gaetano still had the cold, bitter taste in his mouth. He slid his cup away from him.

"No, thank you. I've had enough. But I'll keep you company for a few more minutes," he said as he tapped a cigarette from the pack that Sister Franca had given him. He put it to his lips, lit a match, and fired the tip of the cigarette, then stared at the burning match as he drew in his first lungful of smoke.

"Then I'll go down and put them in the furnace, and hope that they don't scream while they burn."

18

SEBASTIANO SLID HIS HAND along the wall at the top of the basement steps until he found a switch that turned on a single, dim yellow bulb that hung in a cage overhead. The bulb crackled a bit and then fell silent as the boy debated whether to leave the door open or pull it shut. Closed, it would arouse no suspicions. But if he left it open he would not feel quite so alone down there.

He left it open just a few inches and started down, taking the first few steps gingerly, and then picking up his pace. The cellar below him was dark; there was nobody to hear him if he made the stairs creak.

But wasn't there?

No. They're in the box. They're sleeping, he told himself, just so he would keep going. And even if the puppets could hear him, they would know he meant them no harm. All he wanted was Pagliaccio.

As he reached the limits of the sickly yellow illumination from that single bulb at the top of the stairs, he paused. His throat felt as if it were closing. His heart began a rapid thudding in his chest that he felt in his head, as if his brain were thumping right along with it, banging around inside his skull. The blackness filled the basement, flowing at his feet like some silent, wine-dark sea.

And where was the light? He reached the bottom step, felt ahead with the toes of his right foot until he found the stone floor. Had he expected some kind of bottomless pit? Of course not, but he could not escape the sensation that the ground—no, the world—beneath him was unreliable and might at any moment give way, tumbling him into a shadow that had no end, a darkness that would swallow any light that might be brought to bear upon it.

Sebastiano couldn't breathe. He felt very small. Smaller, even, than when he stood beside Father Gaetano. One trembling hand on the railing, he began to turn to run back upstairs, and then he thought of Pagliaccio. The clown had not always reassured him, but he had a way of making things all right, a brusqueness that somehow comforted Sebastiano because it came with an unspoken promise that they would always be friends. Pagliaccio would never abandon him.

He searched for the switch, trying to recall its location, running his hands over the posts at the bottom of the steps but finding nothing. Sebastiano had seen some places where lights were turned on by tugging little metal chains that hung from a fixture, so he took a step forward and waved his hands in the air. Would he be too short to reach, if there were such a chain? He thought the answer would be yes.

Alone in the dark, he froze, unsure how to proceed. The only sounds in the basement were the groaning of the building above him, the hushed roar of the fire burning in the furnace, and the ticking of hot metal. Opening his eyes wide, he tried to let his vision adjust, and was rewarded with a vague gray outline of the boxes and trunks and old furniture stored in the basement. The orange glow around the hatch in the furnace was enough to give him that much at least.

And wasn't that the shape of the puppet theatre, just there, halfway between him and the furnace, draped once again in its old blanket? Father Gaetano and Sister Veronica must have brought it down as well, and the ornate box of puppets must be nearby. Before he could let fear paralyze him, he started toward the theatre, pushing his feet ahead of him, using his toes to search for anything that might be blocking his way. A little frightened voice in his head wondered if there might be rats in the basement. There was a hole in the sock on his left foot and his baby toe stuck out. The little voice thought a rat might like to bite that toe.

But then he had reached the theatre, and his worries about rats were forgotten. He put a hand on the theatre, reached beneath the blanket, and felt the proscenium and the curtain that hung in the opening. He glanced around in the orange-hued darkness, searching for any sign of the puppet box. It must be nearby.

The furnace clicked several times and its shush became a quiet roar, the fire stoking higher inside. Someone had turned up the heat, and it burned louder. He stared at the furnace, blinking, and thought that something had scurried past in the dark. Rats, or his imagination. Or something worse than either of those.

"Pagliaccio?" he whispered, listening hard for any reply, even the most muffled.

A rustling came from the dark. He stared at it, eyes wide, and a shape resolved itself in the dark—a box, with something leaning against it. Releasing his hold on the theatre, he shuffled two steps nearer the furnace, and saw that it was the puppet box after all. The lid was off, leaning against it.

The furnace clicked again, drawing his eye. It burned brighter, and in the orange glow of fire that seeped around the edges of the hatch, he saw small figures moving toward it. Movement blocked out the light at the right-hand edge of the hatch, a level clacked, and the hatch door swung open, throwing light and heat into the basement as the fire roared with this new freedom.

In the firelight, he saw a procession of puppets moving toward the furnace, witches and musketeers and animals dragging two of their own: Noah and Pagliaccio. The prisoners struggled. Noah's wife stood by, head hung, and only watched as her own son held a hand over his father's mouth to keep the puppet silent. Goliath carried Pagliaccio in a murderous embrace, muffling his cries, though the fearful little voice in Sebastiano's head told him that the clown had only stitching for a mouth and that his voice came from somewhere else. And then all logic, even that tiny bit of reason, was obliterated by the sight that greeted him next.

On the tiny iron ledge beside the furnace door, Lucifer stood with his wings spread. They had been singed black on the edges by his nearness to the fire. As the first line of puppets climbed up to that iron ledge, passing Noah hand over hand, they stopped trying to silence him and the old man's voice rang out in fear and protest. He screamed for his wife, who turned away, and for his son, who looked on in grim anticipation.

"He will burn for his sins," Lucifer said. "Put him in."

The devil puppet looked directly at Sebastiano, and the little boy was sure that it smiled.

"I have been cast out," Lucifer said. "And now I am the King of Hell."

Balanced precariously on that iron ledge, the puppets began to feed Noah into the flames. His feet and robes caught first, but the fire spread quickly. As he burned, the puppet cried out to God for salvation.

Something broke inside Sebastiano then. He heard a voice screaming, and somewhere within himself he knew it was his own, but he was barely aware of making the noise as he rushed toward the furnace. He kicked at the puppets carrying Pagliaccio, watching the clown tear himself loose and begin to fight. Then he reached for Noah.

The other puppets attacked him as he grabbed the old-man puppet by the head. Lucifer only laughed as Sebastiano tugged Noah from the furnace, and the little boy realized his mistake in an instant. The puppet was ablaze, burning with a fire now its own, and the flames began to lick at the boy's hand. Screaming in fright and pain, he flung the burning Noah puppet away and watched it strike the old theatre, igniting the blanket that had been hung over it like a shroud.

The fire seemed hungry. It leaped from blanket to curtain to the wood of the theatre, and then to boxes and crates and old pillows stacked around the theatre, all in a matter of moments. The fire roared.

And Lucifer laughed.

Something sharp stabbed Sebastiano's ankle. As he flinched away, his foot caught on Goliath, and then he was falling to the stone floor, with the fire spreading and the puppets rushing at him, their inhuman eyes promising all the torments of Hell.

All the while, Sebastiano kept screaming.

FATHER GAETANO CAME BARRELING DOWN the stairs at such speed that he missed a step, slipped, and fell on his back. He thumped down the last half-dozen steps, but the moment he reached the bottom, he sprang up again. Smoke had begun to fill the basement and he kept his head low as he charged toward the flames.

Somehow the puppets had dragged Sebastiano to the floor, where they crawled all over him. Goliath had found a hammer, and as Father Gaetano rushed toward the fallen boy, the big puppet struck Sebastiano in the face. The boy's scream cut off instantly, and Goliath raised the hammer for another swing, aiming this time for the boy's temple.

With the fire roaring in his ears, flames jumping from box to broken rocking chair to stacks of newspaper bound with twine, Father Gaetano descended upon Goliath. He tore the hammer from the puppet's grasp and flung the tool across the room, into the blaze. Burning wood crackled as the priest grabbed hold of Goliath and tossed him after the hammer, the huge puppet screaming as it burned.

Father Gaetano stepped on a tiger and kicked a musketeer. He reached down, knocked two witches aside, and hauled Sebastiano to his feet. The boy's left cheek was swollen badly from the hammer blow, and he seemed only half-conscious. The priest propped him up and kicked away a puppet that tried to pull on the leg of his trousers.

He didn't ask what Sebastiano thought he was doing, there in the basement. He didn't have to. The boy had come down to retrieve Pagliaccio, perhaps suspecting that he might never have another chance. In the back kitchen, Father Gaetano and Sister Teresa had heard his screams. If Sebastiano had not been screaming so loudly, or if he had closed the basement door all the way instead of leaving it open a few inches, they would not have heard anything until it was too late—both for Sebastiano, and for the orphanage of San Domenico. As it was, the flames were spreading fast, and Father Gaetano blamed himself. He had tried to spare the boy's feelings and almost gotten him, and perhaps many others, killed in the process.

"Come, boy!" he shouted over the roar of fire. "Walk!"

But Sebastiano dragged his feet so that Father Gaetano

had no choice but to throw the boy over his shoulder and carry him toward the stairs.

As he turned away from the fire, he caught sight of two small figures struggling near the furnace. Lucifer, of course. And Pagliaccio. The clown struck the devil, knocking him back toward the furnace's base, and then Pagliaccio stood above him, looking down. Flames spread behind the clown like wings of fire, as if he were the fallen angel, not Lucifer. But then the Devil rose, his wings charred to black stubs, and laughed so loudly that the insidious noise spread through the smoke and the fire, seeming to whisper in Father Gaetano's ears.

Several puppets emerged from the smoke and flame, themselves burning, and reached for Pagliaccio.

The priest tried to tell himself it was only a puppet, but he knew better than that now. With Sebastiano moaning, draped over his shoulder, Father Gaetano rushed back in. The hairs on his arms crinkled and burned and he felt his skin searing as he came so close to the flames that he feared the boy's hair might ignite.

He stomped on the burning puppets, smearing them on the stone floor with a scrape of his shoe, and plucked Pagliaccio from the ground.

Still, Lucifer laughed, and when the priest turned, he saw why. The fire had begun to close in behind him, folded piles of old curtains catching fire, which spread to a small shelf of moldy books.

"Look at you!" Lucifer crowed. "What kind of God cannot even save Himself?"

"I told you!" Father Gaetano shouted, rounding on the devil. "I'm not God! I only held the strings!"

Lucifer glared up at him, the cloth of his body igniting, singeing, and then charring black.

"Perhaps you should have held on to them more tightly," the devil said as he burned.

Shouts filled the basement. Father Gaetano turned away, crouching low with the boy on his shoulder, and tried to see through the encroaching flames. Something splashed and steam rose, and he saw a line of children and nuns throwing buckets of water onto the flames, making him a path to escape. He dashed through the smoking debris and joined them.

Marcello and Sister Veronica took Sebastiano from him. The little boy had struck his head and inhaled too much smoke, but he was half conscious when Father Gaetano tucked the scorched clown puppet into his hand. Marcello and Sister Veronica carried Sebastiano upstairs, out of the smoke, and Father Gaetano took his place in the bucket line. They doused the nearest flames, but when he turned to see Sister Teresa about to throw water onto the blazing ruin of the puppet theatre, he shouted for her to wait.

"Let it burn!" he called.

He held up a hand, gesturing for them all to stay back—to keep the water in their buckets. Long seconds passed during which the hungry fire raged, until Sister Teresa and several of the other nuns began to cry out to him in fear that the whole building would be engulfed.

Only when he felt sure that the last of the puppets had

been burnt to char did he wave them on, and allow the bucket brigade to continue.

Hours later, the last of the cinders had been doused. Of the puppets, all that remained were ashes.

Still, he wondered.

19

YEARS PASSED. The war ended. Sicily, once so desired for its strategic value in the Mediterranean, was abandoned by the world's powers, its significance largely forgotten. Most of the children were adopted by people from the village of Tringale, or claimed by distant relatives once the threat of war had passed. In time, the orphanage became merely a rectory once again. Of the orphans, only one remained. Soon enough there were two priests at the church of San Domenico, and then three, but Father Gaetano was not among them. He had departed even before the war's end.

In Tringale, they still talked about the young priest. The children who had been adopted from the orphanage told stories—wild, incredible tales, equally horrid and absurd—and the story of Father Gaetano's Puppet Catechism became a legend, of sorts. At least in Tringale.

Caretakers came and went. The church's pastor would hire one, and not long after the man would quit the job. Some of them had the decency to apologize, but others simply left at the end of one work day and never returned. The more courteous among them would make a game attempt to muster up some explanation for their abrupt departures, but they needn't have bothered. The priests, and the nuns at the convent, always knew it had been the basement that frightened them off.

The basement, and the furnace.

The fire that burned that December night left many scars behind, both on those who had been there to see it and on the floors and walls. The black scorching on the stone would remain for as long as the rectory stood. Everything that had been stored in the corner by the furnace had been charred to ruin, removed and carted away in the days after the blaze. None of the workers who took part ever volunteered their services to the church of San Domenico again. Several stopped going to mass altogether.

Father Gaetano installed a heavy deadbolt lock with three keys. The pastor had one, the convent's mother superior the second, and the long succession of caretakers would hold the third. They were the only three who were allowed to descend into the basement unaccompanied. In time, the church had a new pastor who kept all three keys for himself. Rumors spread about him, and about the single, scorched puppet that sat on a shelf in his office. Once, so the whispers said, it had been a clown. It was also said that the pastor, Father Sebastiano, would not permit even the caretaker to go into the basement alone, especially when the weather turned cold.

In the winter, when the furnace crackled and hissed with fire, strange noises could be heard amidst the roar of flames. *A sound like the screaming of the damned,* one caretaker claimed, in a note he left behind when he fled his duties in the middle of the night.

As if Hell itself is close by, he wrote.

Just out of reach.